FLYING WITH THE EAGLES

FLYING
WITH THE
EAGLES

Mary Trask

XULON PRESS

Xulon Press
2301 Lucien Way #415
Maitland, FL 32751
407.339.4217
www.xulonpress.com

ISBN-13: 978-1-54565-855-0

DEDICATION PAGE

This book is dedicated to first to my wonderful supportive family: John, Joshua, Jenny, Jeremiah, Liz, Jordan, Natalie and our grandchildren: Claire, Avery, Noelle, Joel, Gilead, and Ty. May your journeys of discovery always be led by the light of the One who has loved you even before the beginning of time.

ACKNOWLEDGEMENTS

I would like to first thank my amazing husband, John, who has stood with me these last 39 years of marriage encouraging me to be all that I was designed to be from before I was born. My special thanks also goes to my dear friend, Dori Olsen who volunteered many hours of proofing, correcting, and offering valuable suggestions in the writing of this manuscript. My appreciation is also extended to Terese Miller, Jim Nightingale, Natalie Trask, and Liz Trask, along with other family members and friends who persevered through early versions of this story offering their input and encouraging me in the writing of this book.

Thank you all so much!

TABLE OF CONTENTS

Chapter One

ENCOUNTERS OF INTRIGUE

The trail leading downward to the peaceful meadow didn't appear to be too steep at first, but her feet slid a bit on the loose gravel strewn on the path. She was glad to finally see the house she had been searching for. Even through the haze, she could see the smoke from the stone chimney lazily drifting into the air above the rustic cabin where she was headed. Relief swept over her as she anticipated delivering Miss Haddie's message.

Miss Haddie had instructed her to deliver the message yesterday. Instead, she had chosen to go home first and continue her mission the following day.

Last night with her father, Oren, had been encouraging and relaxed. He was thrilled with the apple pie she brought home. He didn't even press her about the details of her training under Miss Haddie. All he cared about was Shoshanna's upcoming presentation before the village elders and their evaluation of her for marriage.

Miss Haddie's message would only be delivered one day late. This certainly had been the best choice for all, she reasoned. Even Miss Haddie may have been inclined to make the same decision herself, had she been in her shoes.

As she headed out the door the following morning, she worked to console her guilty conscience with all the good that had been accomplished in spite of this one slight deviation. Her mission was nearly accomplished and obviously, there had been no need for her to rush.

However, just as she was preparing to step out of the surrounding forest, she noticed a group of men coming from the other direction followed by a woman. Even from a distance, Shoshanna could see the woman was clearly upset.

Taking a moment to step back under cover, she watched. The men loudly pounded on the rough wooden door demanding to speak to Galen, the man who was to receive Miss Haddie's message. The door swung open and the group filed in. It wasn't long before the band emerged with Galen handcuffed in their midst as they led him away. His distraught parents stood outside the entrance of the cabin watching and clinging to each other, helpless to do anything to stop them.

Shoshanna's stomach suddenly churned in grief as she realized that her delay in following directions may very well have caused her friend to be arrested and taken away! With guilt and a sense of responsibility weighing heavily upon her, she followed from a distance. She needed to find out where they were taking Galen so she could tell Miss Haddie.

It was hard to imagine how only a few days prior, she had viewed life so differently feeling, depressed and lifeless while living in the stifling haze that covered everything. Now here she was bravely chasing after a group of thugs who had seized her friend! Though very purposeful in her pursuit, she reminded herself to remain hidden or she would certainly be arrested as well.

Trailing behind, she was just able to catch glimpses of the stragglers, assuring she was going the right way. When they finally reached the building where the elders gathered, Shoshanna watched as Galen was thrust before the elders to be officially charged with crimes against the village of Kieran where he lived.

She had seen similar events in her own village of Zera. Shoshanna had no doubt in her mind that every accusation launched against her friend came from the lone woman who boldly entered in to the assembly.

Shortly afterwards, Shoshanna watched as the village enforcers led Galen across the courtyard. They escorted him into a thick, impenetrable building where all dissenters were temporarily held for sentencing. Her heart dropped as she watched the heavy iron doors slam shut and heard the screeching of the lock as it slide into place. She had to get to Miss Haddie on the other side of the island! She would know what to do.

Several days earlier, Shoshanna had awaken with a disturbing dream in the forefront of her mind. Though she couldn't actually recall all the details, she recollected something about climbing the smoking mountains located in the center of the island. The climb itself seemed exhausting, even in her dream! She remembered examining a curious engraving found on a stone. It appeared to be an eagle with outstretched wings.

Suddenly eerie voices shouted in her ears.

"Abandon your climb! This is hopeless! You will only fail again!" As the voices screamed, she felt weak, vulnerable and unable to resist. Something was pushing her from behind directly towards a cliff. As she was falling, she woke up.

Waking up shaking and in a cold sweat, the voices continued to haunt Shoshanna. Pulling herself out of bed, she stumbled over to the window, desperate for the daylight. She brushed her long chestnut hair out of her face. Her rumpled night clothes hung loosely around her shapely petite body. Stretching, she rubbed the sleep from her darkly lashed hazel eyes. The morning sun had already begun to make its grand appearance. Even through the smoky haze, she saw its brilliant display of oranges and reds.

"Time for a walk," she decided, knowing exactly where she needed to go.

The familiar path was heavy with overgrowth, as she fought her way along. Twigs and other obstructions grabbed at her clothing, though the path before her was still visible.

As grueling as it was, this path led to peace, quiet and treasured moments of solitude.

After what felt like hours, she caught a glimpse of what she had worked so hard for...the ocean. This was something special that carried with it the sounds of rhythmic surfs and worlds that lay beyond her reach.

Exhausted by her journey, Shoshanna sat down on a fallen tree. She lifted up the gourd she brought along and eagerly drank the water it held. Here, at last, she could enjoy an undisturbed moment or two of sweet silence. Though her panoramic view of the waters was limited by an endless foggy haze, at least she could see a bit of the sea and imagine its expanse. She dug her toes into the colorful grains of sand and breathed deeply of the salted sea air.

There was something very different about the light breezes coming off the vastness before her. She had long ago discovered that if she focused, she could almost hear voices floating across the waters. On other occasions, sweet harmonic, melodies seemed to be carried by the wind and deposited on the shoreline for her to enjoy.

This gentle ensemble of sounds spoke to something deep within her. Her tormented mind was slowly lulled to a place of rest, as temporary as it might be. That brief reprieve was the very thing she treasured and was worth the energy it required to get there. She was aware of no other way to find what she was seeking.

This huge island of Kumani and its smoldering mountains was surrounded with violent churning waters and just beyond that, huge, snarling volcanic teeth threatened anyone's escape. This incarceration from the worlds beyond had been so lengthy that few could recall a different life. In the place of reality and truth, myths and legends developed to help explain the hopelessness of their predicament.

Kumani was rich in vegetation and wildlife offering its residents ample provision for all their needs. To even discuss the possibility of life beyond what they knew or were familiar with was considered to be an invitation for death and destruction in their lives and was strongly discouraged among the villages.

Life for every child born on the island was carefully plotted out in order to sustain their little world and keep things continuing as they always had been. Young men were assigned as apprentices to be groomed in a trade chosen for them by the village elders. Young women began their preparations at an early age to be wives and homemakers. Their attitudes were carefully manipulated to ensure submission to all authority. Young ladies were expected to marry and assist the man chosen for them. Their world was perfectly planned permitting no interference or dissention.

This was the world Shoshanna had grown up in and the one she desperately desired to be free from.

She had no choices, no freedom, and nothing to look forward to. Their civilization was just as stifling to her as the smoky haze they were forced to breathe every day. She longed for something more…but if asked what that might be, she had no answers.

The voice of her father replayed repeatedly in her mind as she heard him run through the litany of names of those who refused to comply with the system. They either disappeared or suddenly died from no apparent cause. Their devastated families were looked down upon. All orphans were placed in carefully protected training camps where they were re-educated in the proper manners of life so as to contribute to the good of all.

Hours drifted by as Shoshanna pondered her own emptiness while gazing out into the forbidden seas of freedom. An unfamiliar sound to her left suddenly caught her attention. She heard the gentle dipping of an oar in the water followed by the tip of a small canoe emerging from out of the haze. Quickly Shoshanna withdrew back into the dense greenery hiding from the person navigating the craft. The canoe landed not far from where she sat.

A young girl, maybe ten years old, stepped out from the craft lifting out a sack nearly as big as she was. The fair-haired child with a long braid running down her back easily maneuvered both the canoe and the bundle she carried. Once the canoe was secured, she glanced briefly around before heading down a pathway Shoshanna had never noticed before. A strange curiosity compelled her to follow the young adventurer. Trying desperately not to make any noise or draw attention to herself, she kept a short distance between them.

Moving deeper into the forest, Shoshanna encountered several forks in the path. As she hesitated, a rustling in the brush indicated which of the two trails the child had chosen. This happened multiple times until finally Shoshanna came to the outskirts of a homestead where the forest had been cleared. She remained in the shadows so she could carefully survey what lay before her.

The brightly painted cottage had a quaint appearance with flower boxes under each of the shuttered windows and a carefully groomed and thriving vegetable garden. Fruit trees and berry bushes of every sort lined the borders of the clearing. Smoke rose from the stone chimney stack above the home clearly implying that someone was there. Sweet smells of cinnamon and freshly baked apples hung in the air filling her senses with such comfort and longing that she nearly forgot herself and walked right up to the door.

Inlaid in the heavy wooden front door, a beautiful stained glass sunset captivated her attention. Carved into the wood above the inlaid colored glass was a majestic eagle with wings outspread, ready to catch the upward drafts in flight. The scene was mesmerizing, almost appearing alive as she continued to stare.

While studying the door further, Shoshanna suddenly noticed the large burlap sack the child had been carrying slumped over near the entrance. Her heart raced as she realized she had successfully followed the young girl to her destination. As she wondered about the contents of the sack, she heard a slight squeak of the hinges as the front door began to open.

Taking a step backwards into the covering of the trees, she watched as a slightly plump, elderly woman stepped out with the young girl drawn close for protection. Her gray hair twisted in a bun at the nape of her neck. Her blue eyes appeared sharp and clear as they scanned the property for any sign of an intruder. Suddenly, she turned her gaze upon the exact location where Shoshanna hid.

"You there!" she called out. "What is it you want?"

Unsure as to whether to turn and run or reveal herself, Shoshanna suddenly found herself stepping out into the open before the old woman and child. With eyes downcast in humble apology for her intrusion, her words seem to stumble out all over each other.

"I'm…I'm so sorry. I didn't mean to scare the child. I just was curious about where she was going. I didn't mean to bother you. I'll head back now," she concluded while turning back to the trail she had followed. However, she had no idea how she got there or how to return to her "secret" shoreline.

"Wait a moment," the woman responded. "Would you like to join us for tea and bread before you return?"

Glancing back over her shoulder at the two still huddling close, Shoshanna realized the woman was smiling with a gleam in her eyes that literally took her breath away for a moment. A wave of peace and love washed over her weary soul. In response to her kind invitation, the young woman returned the smile. She was tired and the idea of resting for a bit with a cup of tea actually sounded delightful.

Without waiting for a response, the woman spun around gently nudging the child ahead of her as they walked back towards the cottage.

"Come along, then," she called back as they re-entered through the front door.

Unsure at what had just transpired, Shoshanna moved slowly towards the house. Stepping closer towards the cottage, she realized the ever present smoky haze was no longer there. All around the homestead clear skies and bright rays of sun shone through. Now, she really didn't know what to think...but her hosts were waiting, so she stepped closer to the open door.

Chapter Two

A NEW FRIEND

Before Shoshanna had a chance to actually enter the cottage, opposite her, a young man stepped out from the woods carrying firewood. His brawny arms bulged at the weight of his load. Beads of sweat dotted his forehead and dampened his thick, black wavy hair that swept across his brown eyes. Both of them froze, gazing at each other in bewilderment.

"Miss Haddie!" the young man called out, never breaking eye contact. "I have some firewood for you! May I come in?"

Shoshanna watched as he walked through the front door into the home. She heard the woman inside greet him cheerfully.

"Oh Galen, you are so thoughtful! Come in, come in! Would you mind putting the firewood next to the stove, please?"

By this time, Shoshanna had moved close enough to the front door so she could poke her head in through the threshold wondering if she was still welcome. Noticing her reluctance, Miss Haddie beckoned for her to come join them for tea. She timidly approached the table where Miss Haddie and the young girl were already enjoying steaming mugs of tea and fresh, crusty bread glistening with sweet honey.

Galen finished stacking the logs and headed towards the front door.

Looking towards Miss Haddie, he explained, "I noticed some logs that needed splitting. I'm going to take care of that for you, if that is okay."

"My goodness, Galen! You are a blessing! Yes, thank you so much. I appreciate your help...and don't be concerned about our visitor. I have invited her for tea," Miss Haddie smiled.

Nodding, Galen stepped back outside, but not before giving Shoshanna a second glance of warning. He wanted to make sure she knew he was close by and would be watching.

Shoshanna sat down at the table, still feeling quite uncomfortable.

"You must be hungry and thirsty by now. Please, help yourself, my dear."

Shoshanna reached for the tea pot and poured some tea as Miss Haddie continued.

"My name is Miss Haddie, as you already heard and this is young Jessah, one of my very favorites. As you can see, I live alone most of the time, but on occasion, my dear friends come to bring me things and keep me company."

"Jessah has come bearing gifts, as you noticed," she continued. "This dear child often brings me fresh baked bread and other goodies to keep me well supplied."

"Oh, Miss Haddie," Jessah interjected apologetically, "I am so sorry she followed me here, but I felt this was permitted to happen, so I rustled the branches so she could hear me at the forks in the path."

"Yes, yes, Jessah. You were right. She is supposed to be here," Miss Haddie assured her. "And I suppose you have noticed what I am seeing as well? Tell me dear, what do you see?"

Taking a deep breath, Jessah turned her focus on Shoshanna and looked very deeply into her eyes before speaking.

"I see a grey cloud upon her mind. Deep pain, loss. I see a child running away in tears looking for peace."

"Good, good," Miss Haddie encouraged the child. "Your eyes are becoming very clear now. Excellent! What else do you see?"

Meanwhile Shoshanna squirmed as Jessah appeared to look right through her. It seemed as though all her secrets were being exposed causing her to feel very vulnerable before people she barely knew.

"Wait, a moment," Shoshanna interjected. "I didn't really come here for this."

"Oh, of course you didn't. Jessah was just practicing and we are done now," Miss Haddie assured her. "Now we would like to hear more about you, my dear."

Before speaking, Shoshanna took a sip of tea hoping it would calm her nerves.

"My name is Shoshanna. I live with my father in the village of Zera. This morning, I woke up and felt like taking a walk to my favorite beach so I could enjoy some moments of peace. As I was relaxing, I suddenly noticed Jessah landing her canoe near me…so I followed her to see where she was going with that sack. That's all."

"And is that all? Don't you have anything else you want to ask me about?" Miss Haddie prodded her.

Feeling as though she were about to take a plunge into very unfamiliar waters, Shoshanna took a breath to consider whether she wanted to inquire any further. There were several things that caught her attention that she had no natural explanation for. Yes, she needed to understand or she would be upset later with herself simply because she was afraid to ask.

"Okay, so I do have a few questions," she admitted. "My entire life, I have lived with the haze coming from those smoldering mountains. How is it that there is no haze on your homestead at all?"

Just at that moment, Galen popped his head in through the front door.

"I have finished splitting the wood for you outside. Is there anything else I can help you with?"

"Oh no, Galen. Everything is already taken care of. Thank you! Why don't you relax a moment and join us for tea. You have time, don't you?" Miss Haddie inquired.

"Yes, I suppose I could stop and enjoy some tea and that wonderful bread you have," he conceded.

"Come sit here and join us then."

Slowly Galen walked over and pulled out a chair from the table feeling a bit guilty for being so suspicious of the beautiful young woman now sitting beside him. Though he too could see the cloud hanging over her mind at the moment, the hunger crying out in her eyes moved him with compassion.

"Galen, this is Shoshanna from the village of Zera where she lives with her father," Miss Haddie explained. "She followed Jessah from the landing and now wants to know why there is no haze here," she said with a sparkle in her eyes.

Galen extended his hand to their new friend.

"I'm so glad to meet you…and I'm sorry I was a bit suspicious of you when I first arrived."

"Oh, that is fine. I really wasn't sure if all of this was real or I was just dreaming again, so I probably looked very suspicious."

"Let me assure you," Galen stated with clarity, "this is definitely not a dream. It is probably more real than you can imagine."

Unsure of what he was referring to, Shoshanna looked back to Miss Haddie for further explanation. Picking up where they left off, Miss Haddie proceeded to answer Shoshanna's question.

"First, let me explain the clarity around this property. It all has to do with what is going on here," she said touching the side of her head. "If we know what is true, we no longer have to live in shadows. There is quite a bit involved with fully explaining all this, so we might need to move slowly at first, if that is alright."

Now Shoshanna was really confused, but still nodded in assent to what she said.

Turning her attention to young Jessah who was avidly taking all this in, Miss Haddie asked her about her journey to the landing that morning.

"Oh, it was wonderful this morning!" Jessah exclaimed. "When I woke up, I envisioned a door standing open, so I knew it was time for me to come visit you. The sack was setting where it usually is and the canoe was awaiting me in the usual spot. As I traveled here, I noticed the dolphins playing around the canoe, even giving it a little shove every once in a while to make my journey a bit easier. I am certain when I return, my absence will not be noticed at all, just like before."

Shoshanna said nothing, but her eyes grew wider in amazement.

Smiling, Miss Haddie leaned over to hug the young girl.

"You know, you are an amazing child and soon things will change for you. Your time left in the training camp will shortly be coming to an end. I see a new family for you allowing you the freedom to continue growing in truth as you have been."

Giggling with glee, Jessah smiled burying her face into Miss Haddie's embrace. Happily, Jessah returned to nibbling on the slice of sweet bread she had before her.

Next Miss Haddie turned towards Galen who had been listening while eating his bread.

"And what about you?" she asked. "How are your parents doing?"

Taking a sip of tea before he spoke, Galen responded.

"They actually were better for a time as they were drinking the tea you sent over, but since that time, they began listening to their friends again. Once they stopped drinking the tea, their minds grew weak. It's obvious their judgment is easily swayed. The effects of that haze is incessant!"

Galen shared about his parents just as Shoshanna was sipping her own tea. Unsure of what its contents might be and how it might affect her, she decided to set it aside until she learned more about all this.

"I am sorry to hear that, Galen," Miss Haddie replied. "And how do they feel about you visiting me as often as you do?"

Taking another sip of tea, Galen grinned slightly saying, "They don't actually know much about that. They assume I have been working as an apprentice with Jarek, the blacksmith, but instead I have been training in other ways that I feel are far more profitable...like coming to see you!"

Miss Haddie laughed as Galen continued.

"Others have tried to warn me about the "dangers" of not complying with the desires of the village elders and their plans for us all, but I have just not been listening very well, I guess. I keep hearing other voices directing me in a different way. When I respond to the way of the eagles,

I feel so much hope and peace. I know there is no turning back for me."

As Miss Haddie and Jessah smiled, the mention of eagles triggered another question in Shoshanna's mind.

"Yes! Eagles!" Shoshanna chimed in. "What about the eagles? I noticed the one carved in the archway of your home. What does that mean?"

The three looked at each other as they considered how much to tell Shoshanna at that point. Miss Haddie spoke up.

"Child, there is much for you to learn from the eagles that soar high in the air above all that is going on here. With that haze still in place over your mind, you would not be able to comprehend very much right now. There is a much bigger plan in place that you are not yet fully aware of and we must be wise in what we tell you for your own protection."

"All I can tell you now is that you are on the path of discovery. If you continue, many things will change for you. If you withdraw and choose to remain as you are, then you will see us no more. It is up to you entirely. To step into the unknown requires great courage, trust, and the desire to press through adversity in order to become more than you can imagine right now. If you are willing to lay down everything you think you know in exchange for what is true, then we will meet again and continue your training. Until that time, you must deal with your choices. Let us leave it at that."

Miss Haddie stood, indicating their visit was over. As they headed towards the door, Shoshanna turned back towards her new acquaintance saying, "Miss Haddie, I do believe I want more of what you speak of, but I will take the time to consider this fully. However, now that I am here, I honestly am not sure at all how to return to my father's house. Will you be able to direct me back?"

Galen spoke up, "I can guide you back to your village, if you would like."

"Yes, I would greatly appreciate that." Then turning towards Jessah, Shoshanna offered her hand to the child. "It was wonderful meeting…I mean, following you, as you led me here. I really hope I can learn more about you someday. You do sound amazing!" Jessah smiled broadly in response.

With Miss Haddie closely following the group to the door, Shoshanna turned around and hugged her like she had hugged no one else before. She felt as though it were her own mother hugging her in return.

"You have stirred me and challenged me so much. I feel like I am bursting with even more questions, but I know I must wait and consider, and so I will. Thank you for allowing me a glimpse of something that offers me hope. I am confident that we will meet again very soon."

With that, they all stepped out the front door. Miss Haddie stood in the threshold waving as Jessah departed on the path to the left of the homestead, while Galen and Shoshanna took the path just to the right. As they stepped into the foliage, the young woman turned one more time to wave at her new friend, but instead of the homestead, she saw nothing but dense forest behind them.

Looking towards Galen for an explanation, he just shook his head and kept walking ahead.

Chapter Three

CLEARING THINGS UP

Silence reigned between the two for a while as Shoshanna struggled with the idea of probing Galen for more information. Miss Haddie made it clear that there were some things she needed to consider before moving on in her relationship with these three, but at the moment, she wasn't even sure what she should be considering. Finally, she couldn't stand it any longer.

"May I ask you a question," she inquired.

"It depends."

"On what?" Shoshanna was getting a little annoyed with all this secrecy.

"On what you are going to ask me," he replied, smiling as he gave her a side glance.

Trying to ignore her own frustration, she pressed on to see what more she could learn.

"Okay, so Miss Haddie said there was some kind of haze over my mind preventing me from understanding some things. How does she know that? Can she see something I can't see? And if I do have this "haze" over me, how do I get rid of it?"

"That is a really good question," Galen responded, "I'm not sure I can fully explain, but I can try."

As they walked, Galen began describing the basic differences between what they grew up with and what was actually available.

"The mind is like a doorway. If we believe lies, those lies create darkness all around us, preventing us from seeing clearly. If we can't see properly, it's easy to choose things that are actually destructive to us and others. Darkness works to enslave all of us to fear, harmful emotions, and thought patterns."

"You make it sound as though this darkness was alive," she noted, quite puzzled by what he was saying.

"It is quite real, I'm afraid. However at the same time, so is light." He could see Shoshanna was confused at this disclosure. "To help you understand better, let's call light truth and darkness lies. These two are constantly in a battle to persuade people to agree with them. If you agree with darkness or lies, you become its slave. If you agree with light or truth, you become free."

Galen continued.

"Just because we can't see something with our natural eyes or even touch it with our hands does not mean it doesn't exist. For example, can you actually see love, or do you just witness the effects of it on people? How about fear? Must you touch it with your hands in order to validate its existence?"

"In the same way, the source of all lies is very real and attempts to cloud every available mind with darkness. Truth, however is much more powerful as it not only clears the mind, but it also sets people free to live in a way where love is able to be given and received. Truth allows us to soar high just like the eagles!"

Suddenly, Galen stopped himself. "Oh, you don't know about the eagles yet, do you?"

A bit indignant at his insinuation, she replied, "Of course, I know what eagles are. I have seen pictures of them and know that they fly in the air like other birds."

"Well, yes. That is true, but eagles are very different from other types of birds," he explained. "These great birds fly much higher in the sky than any other bird soaring on the winds far above all the smoke and haze surrounding our villages…and that's what truth and light can do in our lives as well."

"You don't mean we can fly like birds, do you?" she asked a bit snidely.

"Not exactly, but there is something about being able to see without all the haze that can make you feel like you are flying sometimes," he added with a smile.

Galen could see she was at her limit of trying to understand it.

"I realize you have much to ponder, as Miss Haddie said, so let's just leave this discussion alone for a while, shall we?"

"Yes, but I do want to know why Miss Haddie said I might not see you again, depending on what choices I make.

I don't know that I am able to fully make the choices I want at this point in my life," she lamented. "You know how life is structured for us in the villages, right? The elders make decisions and we must live with it. I have no choice in this at all!"

"You really believe you have no choice at all?"

"No, of course I don't. Suitable men are given wives as the elders choose. There is no other way. It's for the good of our village and the survival of Kumani!"

"Really?" Galen challenged her. "Is that just what you've been told or is that what is really true?"

Confused, Shoshanna stopped walking and gave him a good hard look.

"What exactly are you suggesting?"

"I am suggesting you take a look at what is true and what is not. This is where you must make a hard decision to determine which way you need to go. It is up to you, not others."

Eye to eye, the two looked at each other for a moment before Galen spoke again.

"We have arrived."

"Arrived?"

"Yes. This is Zera, your village. Right?"

Stunned, Shoshanna looked around her. Yes, she was home. As she glanced back at Galen, she saw him turn and head back into the forest. There were so many more questions whirling around in her head now, she felt completely unsure about her life up to this point and even if she really knew anything.

"Shoshanna!"

The young woman turned back around to see her father, Oren practically running towards her on the path located on the outskirts of Zera.

"Where have you been? I have been watching for you all day!"

"Oh, I just really needed some time alone, so I went for a walk," she explained, not wanting to elaborate.

"Well, it's nearly supper time. I made something for us to eat. Let's go home now. I have much to tell you."

Reluctantly, Shoshanna followed her father back through the suffocating smoke to the cabin they called home, but not before taking a second glance into the forest where Galen had retreated. There was no sign of him. She was back into the only world she really knew, but discontent was already stirring within.

As they walked home she was glad her father was uncharacteristically quiet. This gave her a chance to mull over her conversation with Galen. Suddenly, it dawned on her. Their hike back from the hidden homestead had actually been a rather short walk before they arrived at her village...much shorter than it should have been. How did they cover that distance so quickly?

Now she really felt confused!

Glancing towards her father with his concentrated scowl, she knew it was far better not to mention any of these things to him. He was obviously troubled about something.

Chapter Four

UNDERCOVER OF LIGHT

After paddling the canoe back down the shoreline for some distance, Jessah finally returned to the location from which she embarked on her journey. The inlet, with its strategically positioned trees and their low-hanging branches allowed her, with a slight duck of her head, to glide in and land her craft easily upon its sandy beach.

Within minutes, the canoe was secured and the young girl jumped out and began her trek up the trail leading to Camp Shabelle where the reeducation of orphaned children took place. Once her hike began, Jessah noticed the dreariness of the smoky haze began closing in around her once again. She was glad to see that the light she had become dependent upon was still shining before her leading the way she was to go.

Both the light and the trail weaved back and forth through vegetation until she arrived at the "fortress" she was forced to call home…for now. She swallowed a bit in nervousness trying to moisten her dry throat as she walked up to the huge wooden door she had found opened earlier that day. Now it was late afternoon and both educators and their "trainees" were certain to be moving about by now.

Reminding herself once again about the "light" she had come to know and trust, she cautiously pulled upon the heavy iron ring causing the door to slowly swing towards her. Inch by inch, she tugged at the heavy beamed door praying it would not creak alerting any of the staff to her secret entrance and portal of escape. Once the opening was just big enough for her small body to slip through, she moved quickly to step inside shutting the door behind her.

The darkened hallway was the perfect spot for her to blend in while she awaited her opportunity to quickly rejoin the group she was supposed to have been with all day. Taking a quick peek behind her shoulder, she was relieved to see the huge door had vanished once again and her secret access to the outside was safely hidden.

Her pounding heart felt like a drum loudly announcing her return.

"It will be okay, it will be okay," she assured herself. Taking a deep breath and closing her eyes, she focused on the inner voice directing her next move.

"Wait for a few more minutes, and then you will see your class," the voice instructed her.

After taking a moment to relax, Jessah reopened her eyes to look around again. Coming down the darkened hallway was Miss Moselle, stern and focused, leading a group of girls right past her! She froze and held her breath as they marched by. The line of girls filed directly in front of her as if she wasn't there. Once the group strode past her, she quickly joined the column of girls at the end as if she had been marching with them the entire time.

Only one child noticed Jessah's return to her class. It was her best friend, Yona, who turned her head briefly glancing back at her adventurous friend. When the moment was right, Yona turned and whispered, "Where have you been?"

Smiling, Jessah responded, "Just visiting friends. Did she miss me?" referring to the overly-strict teacher now leading the pack.

"No. She didn't seem to notice that you were gone at all! Why is that?"

Suddenly, a clearing of the throat seemed to indicate that Miss Moselle was aware of the whispering going on at the end of the line so the girls quickly ended their brief conversation. From there, they were all led to their next room where their training and preparation for a "successful reentry" into the outside world continued.

It was nightfall by the time Jessah and Yona had a chance to continue their discussion in private. Lights were off and most of the other girls were already breathing deeply, as they slept. Lying on the top bunk above, Yona poked her head over the side with her long, brown hair cascading down around her cheerful face.

"So tell me! What did you do today? I'm dying to know."

Jessah smiled at her friend's obvious curiosity.

"I went out to the canoe, rowed along the shoreline for a while, and then followed a path to see a dear friend or two."

"Ok, so you are leaving things out on purpose because you don't want me to know how you got out and how you just happened to know where this canoe was. And after your visit, how you were able to return to Camp Shabelle undetected and rejoin us as if nothing happened? That is not normal! Come on. I'm your best friend! Why can't you tell me what is really going on? Do you have a connection with one of the security guards who lets you in and out whenever you want?"

Taking a moment to consider her friend's interrogation, she decided it was time to share some of what she knew.

"No, it's not any connection I have with the staff here. That is for sure! Actually, all of this is pretty normal for me now…ever since I met Elemet one night after my parents died."

"Who is Elemet?"

"He is the one who made all things. He saw my grief and fears, came to me and told me he loved me."

Yona's eyes widened as she considered what Jessah was saying. Jessah continued.

"I know it seems crazy to think someone like that would even notice me, much less speak to me…but he did."

"How did you know it was him?"

"Well first, I was surrounded by light. He told me who he was and then this incredible love just started to penetrate every part of me. It was so wonderful! I just cried and laughed as his love surged through me. I couldn't even talk for a while! Later, I was able to talk to an older friend about what happened…"

"You mean the one you went to see today?"

"Ok, yes. That was the friend I went to see today. I told her about my experience…and she said she had the same kind of thing happen to her many years ago."

"So how has this changed you?" Yona inquired.

"All my fears just melted away. I was not worried about my future anymore, though I knew I still had to live in Camp Shabelle for a while. I knew he would direct me on what to do, what to say, and where to go. And he has done just that!"

"So you have heard His voice more than one time?" she asked incredulously.

"Oh yes, and I see lights directing my path as well."

Yona's heart was beating so hard from what she was hearing, she had to lay her head back down for a moment to consider the magnitude of what Jessah was telling her.

"Do you think he might speak to me as well sometime?" she whispered almost in unbelief.

"I'm sure he will," Jessah replied confidently.

Suddenly, the dorm room door opened as one of their caregivers peeked in to see who was still talking at such a late hour.

"Girls, it's time to sleep now! No more talking!" she called into the room.

"Good night," Yona whispered back. "I'll be dreaming about this all night!"

Chapter Five

A CONFRONTATION OF TRUTH

The door creaked as Galen stepped into his parents' home, expecting a nice supper as usual, but instead his parents, Giza and Eber, were sitting with their friend, Jarek, in the living area obviously waiting for him. Galen stopped stunned at the door gazing at what appeared to be three conspirators plotting his demise.

Giza, his mother, spoke first. "Jarek decided to stop by to see what had become of you. He says you have not been working at his shop as we assumed you were."

"Do you mind telling us where you have been all these many days?" his father chimed in.

Galen, taking a breath, shut the door behind him and then stepped up close to Jarek with his hand outstretched.

"Good evening, Jarek. I'm so glad you came over to see us. I have been meaning to let you know, I have found other employment and am currently in training right now," he said shaking Jarek's hand with a smile.

Now it was Giza and Eber's turn to be stunned.

"Oh, that is fine, son. I actually have taken on another apprentice who is showing great potential as a blacksmith," Jarek responded. "I just needed to find out what had become of you, especially after the village elders had told me to expect you."

"Yes, I should have notified you about the changes. I apologize."

"No problem, young man. I'm glad it's working out for you. Well, now that this has been cleared up, I best be moving on to my home," Jarek said as he stood up and headed for the door. "I am sure my wife has something wonderful prepared for dinner and I am hungry. Good to see you, Eber and Giza. We'll talk again some time."

As Jarek walked out the door and down the footpath, Galen followed him back outside to see him off.

"By the way, who is your new apprentice?"

Continuing his trek in the direction of his home, Jarek merely turned his head aside and called back in response.

"Roany." He was obviously in a hurry to eat.

"Roany?" the young man repeated questioningly.

"Yes, Roany. See you later."

Galen turned back into the house where he was met with two sets of eyes staring him down and awaiting an explanation. Eber spoke first and he was in no mood for vague responses.

"So do you want to tell us about this other employment and the training you are getting?" he asked with raised eyebrows.

Slowly shutting the door behind him, Galen took a deep breath before responding.

"I'm learning how to fly."

"Fly?" his mother gasped. "What are you talking about? No one flies around here except for the birds."

"And eagles." Galen muttered under his breath.

"This is ridiculous," Eber stormed. "You have walked away from a perfectly good apprenticeship and allowed someone else to take your position. How are you ever going to get a wife if you have not acquired the skills needed for your trade? The village elders would never consider your petition for a suitable wife!"

"Dad, I have found a much better way of life than all of that...and I am being trained."

"By whom? Who is teaching you to fly?"

"Have you been visiting with that Miss Haddie again?" Giza asked. "Adina tells me there are some strange ideas coming from this Miss Haddie and that we shouldn't listen to her. And neither should you!"

"And what does Adina know about Miss Haddie?" Galen asked.

"Well, she has heard things, rumors that don't sound right or good." Galen stood upright and looked straight into his mother's eyes hoping to make real contact with her.

"Just so you know, Miss Haddie is a sweet, older woman who needs some assistance around her house every so often and I am honored to help her when I can. Unfortunately, there are people who thrive on rumors and false reports. I'm sorry that Adina has filled your minds with these fables. It is much better to know the facts and not let gossip sway your opinion of someone you barely know. All Miss Haddie has done is send you some of her sweet herbal tea she prepared to help keep your strength up. That does not come across to me as something strange, but rather something kind."

Giza and Eber glanced at each other, feeling a little guilty about their accusations of Miss Haddie. They didn't really know her and the truth was, she had only shown them kindness.

Galen paused and gathered his thoughts for a moment before announcing his intentions for the rest of the evening. "I am heading out again. I have someone I need to see."

"But what about supper?" his mother objected. "You have only just arrived."

"I'm not really hungry right now. I'll be back later. You needn't wait up for me," he stated as he walked back out into the night air.

As he shut the door behind him, the couple looked at each other again, a bit stunned at what had just transpired. Eber spoke first. "Did he ever explain who was teaching him to fly?"

Giza just shook her head and got up deciding it was time for both of them to eat their dinner.

Meanwhile, Galen walked quickly down the footpaths of his village to the home of his closest childhood friend, Roany. Knocking on the wooden door, he waited impatiently for someone to answer.

Finally, Roany's mother, Tanzi, came to the door.

"Galen, what are you doing here? Isn't it a bit late for a visit?"

"Yes, I know it is a little late, but I really need to speak to Roany tonight. Is he here?"

"Oh yes, he's in his room. He's been working hard as an apprentice blacksmith for Jarek. Did you hear about that? So proud of my boy! That's a great skill to master."

"Yes, ma'am. May I speak with him, please?"

"Certainly! You just go ahead and knock on his door. He'll be glad to see you!"

Galen walked across the living area and down the hall to Roany's room and rapped on the bedroom door. Roany opened the door rather sleepily and was a bit surprised to see his friend rather than his mother.

"Galen!"

"I need to talk to you."

"Okay. Come on in." Shutting the door behind him, the young man stretched while yawning as he wearily sat on the bed facing his friend. His curly brown hair was tousled and unkempt as he had obviously had a long hard day of work and was ready to retire for the night.

Once the door was shut, Galen spoke in a half-whispered tone.

"What are you doing?"

"What are you talking about? I'm getting ready for bed. That's what I'm doing."

"No, I'm talking about taking an apprenticeship with Jarek."

"And what is wrong with that?" Roany countered. "Oh, I know what this is about! You are upset because I took your apprenticeship position when you didn't show up. Right?"

"No. I'm not interested in being a blacksmith at all. I'm just confused. I thought you were planning on exploring the smoking mountains with me. I know we spoke about the control of the village elders and this whole silly system. Right?"

"We did."

"So now, what are you doing getting all involved by becoming an apprentice for a blacksmith? That's not who you are! That's not what you dreamed about becoming when we were kids."

"I know, but I'm getting a lot of pressure from people around me to start the process so I can finally be married."

"Is that your mother you are referring to?"

Glancing downward, a bit ashamed, Roany was hesitant to answer.

"Roany, you and I both know you were made to be something much bigger and better than a blacksmith."

"I know that," he admitted, "but I'm not sure what to tell my mother. You know how she is. I just couldn't take any more of her constant pressure. She only has me now and the thought of disappointing her is difficult. I hoped that if I work as a blacksmith for a while, she might ease off me. She doesn't understand any other way. It's hard to convince her of anything beyond what she has believed her whole life."

"That may be true, but are you willing to let go of a future that is free from all this just to pacify your mother?"

"I don't know right now. All I know is I am very tired and I have a lot to do in the morning."

"I'm sure you do. I just don't want to see the real Roany be swallowed up in a world full of dream-killing obligations and mind-numbing control."

"You are probably right."

"I know I'm right. I'm sorry the pressures have forced you into this decision. I just want you to remember the bigger picture and realize you don't have to live this way. I'm just learning more about it myself. We can explore this together, can't we?"

"I hope so."

"I am hoping as well. I guess I'll be leaving now. Get some rest."

"I will. Thanks!"

As Galen stepped out of Roany's room, he thought he saw Tanzi move quickly away from the bedroom door. She hid herself around the corner as if she were working in the kitchen. Galen kept walking to the door and called out "goodbye" as he stepped back out into the smoky haze of the village.

There was a lot on his mind as he slowly meandered his way back to his parents' home.

Chapter Six

TIME FOR A DECISION

Oren opened the door for Shoshanna and pointed to the roughly hewn chair he wanted her to sit in. Shoshanna took a deep breath hoping that she would be able to handle whatever this grim news her father had for her. Sitting directly across from her, he briefly glanced in her direction as he worked to organize his thoughts before speaking. His resolve was obvious, and this only added to the tension already present in the room.

"Shoshanna, I met with the elders of the village today. The time has come for you to join the group of eligible young women who will be matched with those petitioning for a wife."

Stunned, the young woman was unsure on how to respond at first.

"What?" Tears welled up in her eyes as she imagined herself being paraded in front of the elders and petitioners like merchandise. "I'm not ready for something like that. I am just beginning to find out who I really am. I don't want to be given to someone based upon what they want. What about what I want?"

"You have known your entire life that this is the way things are done on Kumani. In order for us to survive, we must listen to and follow the decisions of the elders," Oren reminded her solemnly. "They know what's best."

Silence reigned in the room for several moments as Shoshanna desperately considered all of her options. She had just tasted briefly of something that gave her hope for a different type of life and desperately wanted to find out more about this. It seemed as though the snare had been set and she was being forced to walk into it.

"If mother were here, she would not be forcing me to be marry so soon, and definitely not in this manner!"

Deep sorrow came over Oren's heavily lined face at the mention of his deceased wife. Wearily he ran his hands through his thinning hair. He had suffered much anguish over the loss of his partner in recent years. All the memories of her and her resistance to the ways of the island came rushing back. His dark eyes teared up. If only she had listened to him.

He had tried to counsel her about the dangers of exploring other ways of living outside of what was expected. She had asked questions that shouldn't have been asked and challenged people when she should have remained quiet. He had been afraid for her and watched in great sorrow as she suddenly took ill.

Everyone knew it was her boldness and her inquisitiveness that brought about the changes in her health. This consequence followed all those who dared defy the authorities of the region. After suffering as he did at her loss, he determined that it would not be the same with his precious Shoshanna. He would make sure she was doing all she needed to do to survive and be productive as someone's wife. Even if she would belong to another man, at least she would still be nearby.

In his mind, this was the only way.

"Your mother is no longer here because she resisted the elders on this island," he solemnly reminded her. "I will not allow you to suffer that same fate. The elders have decided it is time for you to begin your marriage preparations. I'm sorry."

Huge tears ran down her cheeks as she stared in unbelief at her father. His compliance felt more like betrayal stabbing her in the heart. He continued.

"You have a few months to prepare yourself for the presentation ceremony. You know what this entails: an examination by Lior, the midwife pronouncing you healthy for childbearing, a demonstration of your baking and cooking skills before the petitioners, and then comely attire that will accent your beauty. We need to begin preparations now."

Shoshanna's mind raced.

With only a few months left of freedom, she had to quickly come up with a resolution to this situation. Realizing her father would not budge in following the decision of the elders, she needed to find an answer that didn't require her be put on display and given to whoever the elders chose.

Suddenly Miss Haddie came to mind. Surely she would know how to escape this nightmarish scenario. Recalling the mysterious encounters she had had earlier that day, Shoshanna suddenly remembered the sweet scent of cinnamon and baked apples coming from the cottage. Maybe that alluring aroma was an indication of Miss Haddie's baking skills and a wonderful excuse for her to receive the wise counsel she needed. Taking a breath while wiping her tears away, she attempted to appear as if she was yielding to his decision.

With her eyes still downcast, Shoshanna responded as respectfully as she could.

"Father, I know you love me and I'm sure that if you knew any other way, you would choose that for me. However, it seems we have no other options. I suppose all I can do now is begin preparing for the presentation ceremony."

Taking a moment to study his reaction, Shoshanna continued, "However, I do feel as though my baking skills are really not what they should be. Without mother here, I haven't had anyone to properly train me."

Oren had to agree. Without his wife around to show Shoshanna the fine art of baking, in recent times, her cooking often looked more like a burnt offering than edible food.

Shoshanna carried on with her appeal. "I recently met an older woman who is skilled in baking that I would like to spend time with so I can improve my abilities. That would be alright, wouldn't it?"

Oren stared for a moment at his beautiful daughter. Even as they discussed the necessary preparations for her presentation, it suddenly dawned on him that he would also be losing his only companion at home. This saddened him even further, but what choice did they have? Shoshanna was strong and able to survive this monumental change in her life, he consoled himself.

She had to!

"Well yes, I suppose getting some more training to help you bake properly might be a wise move. Where is this older woman you speak of? Is she here in Zera?"

"No, not in our village, but in another region, not too far away. I met her on one of my morning walks," Shoshanna explained. "She makes fabulous apple pies, a skill I would like to improve upon. I'm sure she could help in guiding me through this and in all the other areas of cooking and housekeeping I need some improvement in."

"Yes, yes. That makes perfect sense," Oren agreed. "Okay, now that all this is settled, I think it's time for us to enjoy our supper and celebrate your new upcoming life and marriage. I made some beef stew for us, fresh from my butcher shop."

"Oh, that sounds wonderful," Shoshanna responded half-heartedly. Her stomach was still in knots and she was not really hungry at all, but decided it was important for her to keep up appearances of complying. The sudden changes taking place in her life left her feeling stunned, but she still managed to eat some with her father as he babbled on about all his various customers throughout the day. She nodded and smiled as though she were interested in everything he said, but her mind was racing elsewhere.

Oren was obviously relieved, but Shoshanna had many other things to consider. She really didn't know Miss Haddie that well. She only hoped this woman might be able to help her, and then there was the challenge of locating Miss Haddie's homestead again. All those twists and turns on the trail had left her clueless on the correct path to the woman she hoped might be her savior in this situation. Surely, Miss Haddie would have an answer to this terrible predicament forced upon her by the village elders and now, by her own father as well.

It was quite late before Shoshanna was able to quiet her thoughts enough to begin pondering her options once more before morning. Panic was trying to press its way in, but something new was at work telling her that she had the answers needed for all these forced changes.

So what did she already know?

Carefully she considered what she had learned that morning. She remembered the lack of haze around that homestead and how Miss Haddie had suggested that how her thoughts could affect what was around her. Jessah spoke of doors left open for her to walk through and a canoe waiting for her filled with supplies for Miss Haddie. Her walk home with Galen appeared to be much quicker than it should have been with all the distance that had been traveled.

Everything she saw and heard that day seemed to indicate that uncommon things were happening on a regular basis for these people. She, on the other hand, had been brought up believing there were no other options for people on the island of Kumani. Everyone had to follow protocol or suffer the consequences. And yet, with all this understanding, when it came to her continuing to live like everyone else (at least the "normal" people), everything within her screamed in revolt.

Though she had only just met Miss Haddie, she instinctively knew this woman had access to wisdom beyond what she had ever known and could possibly give her the answers to her current dilemma. The way back to the homestead was very unclear, but somehow she hoped that something uncommon would occur for her as well if she put forth the effort to reconnect with Miss Haddie.

At least she had to try.

Chapter Seven

IT'S UP TO YOU

Shoshanna woke up with a start as Galen's words from the previous day floated around in her mind.

"It's up to you, not others."

This phrase replayed over and over again as she struggled to shake the sleep from head. What in the world does that mean? she wondered silently. Then, remembering the great task before her, she sat up. Today was the day she would either experience something "uncommon" or possibly remain lost in the forests of Kumani for some time.

Her heart pounded in nervousness as she mulled over everything she knew one more time. Rising from her bed, she drew back the well-worn curtains. Yes, everything was still covered under the familiar haze. The sun was just peeking over the horizon allowing her plenty of time to pack up a few necessary things. Timing was important as she wanted to leave before her father got up. She would prefer not explaining her journeys any further.

After loading up her knapsack with basic supplies, Shoshanna left a simple note for her father so he wouldn't be concerned. Placing the note on the table, she quietly slipped out the door heading directly for the trail leading to the beach she often visited. This part of her journey did not worry her at all. It was the second part of the expedition that caused her heart to flutter, but she was determined to find Miss Haddie's homestead, if possible.

After miles of pushing aside foliage and ducking under branches, she finally arrived at the beach. The ocean waves gently sketched coastline images upon the sand with fragments of seaweed and broken shells greeting her as she approached. Part of her just wanted to remain. Here, life seemed so easy with nothing but the water, sand, and shells to interact with. However, at the same time, she also knew if she did not press beyond what was comfortable, she would never find the answers she desperately needed.

Looking down the beach, Shoshanna recognized the location where she first saw young Jessah disembark from her canoe. Walking over to the exact spot, she took a moment to examine the vegetation directly in front of the landing. Nothing appeared to indicate any kind of trail leading elsewhere.

A bit frustrated at first, the young woman decided to close her eyes, attempting to imagine where Jessah's foot trail began. After picturing the whole scene in her mind's eye, she was led to look a bit further to her right in the dense vegetation. Meticulously, she moved aside the undergrowth just enough before her revealing the trail she had been looking for. Overjoyed at her discovery, new resolution flooded in as she began her journey of hope and adventure.

At first, the trail was clear and easy to follow, but eventually she came to one of those worrisome forks in which she had to decide which way to go. Studying the two choices, she noted that both were equally worn and neither seemed to give a clear indication as to the correct choice.

This was that moment she had feared.

She stood bewildered while considering which way to go. Her imaginative recall of Jessah's landing had helped her discover the beginning of the trail she needed to follow. Wondering if shutting her eyes would help in this situation as well, she decided to give it a try.

Closing her eyes again, she tried with all her might to bring back any memory of the turns Jessah might have taken at this point, but nothing came to her. With her eyes still shut, she thought back to what she had learned listening to both Galen and Jessah speak about how a light appeared and led them at times. She recalled Jessah describing the grey cloud over her mind when she first sat in Miss Haddie's home. Maybe it was that grey cloud, much like the hazy midst resting upon the villages of Kumani that was preventing her from receiving the clarity she needed at this moment.

Unsure of how to remove the darkness over her mind, she decided to make an appeal to the source of truth or light to help her. Silently, she petitioned for help. While standing in that place of decision, she suddenly felt a stirring deep within her, as if something new was being awakened. It felt as though something from the middle portion of her body rose up within her. She allowed this new feeling of love and life to permeate every part of her before attempting to reopen her eyes once more.

When her eyes did open, it took a moment for them to readjust to the light. Once accustomed to the daylight, things appeared quite differently before her. Though the haze was still present throughout the forest, the trail leading to the right was amazingly clear and free of smoke with a slight illumination about it, while the trail on the left remained clouded over. This was exactly what she needed. An uncommon indicator!

With her confidence moving to a whole new level, she stepped to the right and continued her trek towards the homestead. Left, right, right, left, she followed the clear paths before her until she finally arrived at the mysterious homestead now standing before her as a beacon of light.

Unsure of how to best announce her arrival, Shoshanna stepped out into the clearing cautiously and called out as she had seen Galen do when he arrived the last time.

"Miss Haddie!" she called out. "I'm sorry to disturb you, but I am really in need of your help! Are you here?"

As the front door swung open, aromas of cinnamon and apples filled the air, just as it had the first time she stepped onto the homestead. Shoshanna's lungs eagerly sucked in both the aromas and fresh air as Miss Haddie stepped out. Smiling, Miss Haddie was obviously pleased to see her again.

"Of course I am, my dear!" she responded with a grin. "I have been expecting you. Come in and sit with me. We have much to talk about."

Once inside her comfortable home, Shoshanna was able to better examine the fine furniture and elegant burning lamps set around the cottage. She was surprised she missed so many details during her previous visit. White eyelet curtains hung from her windows allowing the vibrant flowers growing outside to peer through the window panes. Paintings that appeared almost other worldly hung upon her walls, but the one that most caught her attention was that of a beautiful golden eagle soaring through the bright blue skies she had never seen before. That view took her breath away.

Shortly Miss Haddie returned to the table with tea for both of them. Once the delicate tea cups were set down, she sat upon her cushioned seat so she could visit with her guest. However, before giving Shoshanna opportunity to share the purpose of her visit, the old woman took note of some changes in her appearance.

"My dear, you look different today," she commented. "I see some choices have been made which allowed you to find me again. Is this true?"

"Yes! I knew I needed to meet with you today. I was able find the trail Jessah used from the beach to arrive at your home, but when I came to that first fork, I had no idea which way to go. I closed my eyes and then asked the source of truth and light to help me. He did, and I was able to find my way here."

"That is wonderful, Shoshanna! Have you noticed anything different in you and how things appear outside?"

"Oh yes! I saw the light the others were talking about and felt something new inside me as well."

"Yes, my dear. All things are becoming new for you. We can discuss this further later, but first tell me the real purpose of your visit today."

It didn't take long for Shoshanna to begin unloading all the worries and concerns facing her since her selection by the village elders to be added to the list of potential wives.

"I don't want to be chosen like a slab of meat hanging in a shop," she lamented. "My father believes there is no other option other than complete submission, but that's not what I want! I have now seen and experienced evidence of an uncommon way to live. I don't think I can go back and surrender to that old way any longer, but what choice do I have?"

"But child, you have already chosen," Miss Haddie responded. "Don't you see that even making the difficult journey here is an indication that you have begun following that which is truth and light before you? You have chosen the better way and will not be forced to go back to darkness, if you continue to choose light."

"So what do I tell my father?"

"You don't need to tell him anything right now," Miss Haddie continued. "You are in preparation, just as you said, and he will not question you any further at this time."

Shoshanna was taken back for a moment. How did Miss Haddie know what she had told her father in the privacy of their home? This was obviously another of those uncommon things she needed to learn more about. Excitement rose up in her at the prospect of seeing things differently than before. Hungry and ready for change, she began probing her teacher for more.

Questions and answers flowed back and forth between the two as Miss Haddie gave her the history of the island and how things had grown to its current state of haziness and control. Shoshanna was shocked and indignant at times as she learned of the audacity demonstrated by the village elders and their real purposes in establishing such control over the island residents.

By the time, they finished, Shoshanna was thoroughly disgusted with the whole system.

"How could people make such ridiculous choices?" she enquired. "It doesn't even make sense to choose as they did."

"My dear, when haziness and darkness dominate a mind, people are unable to clearly discern anything properly," Miss Haddie explained. "And now I have two things I must have you take care of for me."

"Oh, of course! What do you need me to do?"

Standing up, the woman walked over to her oven and pulled out a freshly baked apple pie and set it on the table in front of her. That explained the wonderful smells of apples and cinnamon Shoshanna encountered when she returned to the homestead.

"I need you to first, deliver this apple pie to your father letting him know that your preparation is going well."

Shoshanna smiled as she gazed upon the perfect pie, knowing this first assignment would be quite easy for her to accomplish. Her father would be so pleased with her preparation that he would gladly encourage her to continue. Then Miss Haddie proceeded.

"After delivering the pie to your home, I need you to travel to Galen's home in Kieran. Please let him know it is time for him to move to the "Eagles' Nest." He knows what that means."

This second request left Shoshanna a bit overwhelmed. She had no idea where the village of Kieran was located nor where Galen lived.

"But Miss Haddie, how do you expect me to find both the village and Galen's home?"

"You found me without knowing the way, right?"

Shoshanna had to agree. The light led her here.

"Then in the same way, the light will lead you in the way you need to go," she assured her.

"But I don't feel like I am ready for a journey of this magnitude," Shoshanna objected. "I just barely have gained some clarity. I think I need more time."

"Dear, we never feel like we are ready for any new challenges. It is only when we allow our abilities to be tested that we will find our confidence and skill increasing."

"But Miss Haddie, why am I needed to tell Galen something if he has the ability to receive direction for himself?"

"My child, it's not that we are needed as much as we are granted the privilege of being a part of this grand adventure of discovery. You have chosen to follow the light you were given and now you are offered the opportunity to follow the light further. Understand?"

"I think so," Shoshanna replied, though she still felt a bit unsure about all this.

"You will be fine. Now, you need to go and do these things for me. You can come again tomorrow, if you like. There is still much for you to learn."

Getting up from the table, Miss Haddie provided a small basket for Shoshanna to carry the pie with and then walked her to the door. As the young woman stepped outside, she turned once more to thank Miss Haddie before walking towards the trail leading to her home.

Her heart was beating both in excitement and nervousness as she practiced following the light once again, leading to her first destination.

Chapter Eight

WHAT NOW?

In less than 24 hours of time, Shoshanna's emotions went from the excitement of being sent out on an assignment to outright grief and regret as she arrived that morning to deliver Miss Haddie's warning to Galen. Though she did come, she had delayed her trip to Kieran as she decided resting at home that evening would allow her to get a fresh start the following morning.

As things turned out, however, there obviously had been a clear purpose behind Miss Haddie's directions. It would have been far better for her to have continued on from her home to the village of Kieran that same day. Now all she could do was stand and watch in horror as men from the village led Galen away in handcuffs.

With remorse still washing over her, Shoshanna decided to track the group from a distance through the forest. She watched as they eventually arrived in the village where her friend was then led into the building where the village elders met. The meeting and ultimate decision in the matter was very brief as Galen, still in handcuffs, was guided across the road to a heavily reinforced prison reserved for dissenters and troublemakers.

Once she knew where he had been taken, Shoshanna moved as quickly as she could back to the other side of the island so she could report to Miss Haddie. She knew this was her fault and felt terrible about the whole mess. She was unsure what kind of response she would get from Miss Haddie, but knew she had to do what she could to help, whatever that might be.

Meanwhile, in the confines of Camp Shabelle, Jessah and her friend, Yona, had just finished breakfast inside the bleak walls of their mess hall, when a rather timid-looking girl informed Yona that she was being summoned by the camp director, Miss Moselle. She was directed to come to the office immediately. Panic-struck, Yona glanced over at Jessah.

"What would she want with me?" Yona asked her friend, basically ignoring the one delivering the message.

"Oh, it's probably nothing," Jessah responded while trying to keep calm herself.

However, the young girl clearly understood the importance of responding to a "request" coming from the camp director. "Miss Moselle said she would like to see you immediately," she emphasized once again.

Noting the urgency of the messenger's tone and facial expressions silently begging Yona to come without delay, Jessah encouraged her to go and find out what Miss Moselle wanted.

"You are nearly twelve," Jessah reminded her. "Maybe it's just time for you to move up into another group."

"I don't want to move to another group," she lamented. "I was just beginning to learn about…"

"Weaving!" Jessah interrupted cautioning her friend with her eyes. "You were just learning how to weave. Right?"

"Oh, yes! Weaving. I was just learning how to weave," Yona agreed. "Well, I guess I better go and find out what this is all about."

Without further delay, Yona got up from the table and turned to follow the young girl to the office. As the girls walked off, Jessah quickly quieted her own concerns enabling her to listen more effectively. Once she focused, peace flooded her heart. She knew Yona would be fine, but she was aware of something else brewing in another location.

Realizing there may be a change in her daily activities, Jessah waited impatiently for dismissal so she could learn what Elemet had planned for her. Table by table, with boys on one side of the room and girls on the other, the children were dismissed so they could clean up and prepare for their day of training and education. Eventually Jessah's table was allowed to exit the room and head for their dorm rooms.

When Jessah arrived back to the dorm, she dove under her bed covers to give her the privacy she needed for her time with Elemet. As she waited, instructions were given.

Before too long, Yona arrived back to the room obviously upset. Hearing the door open and then shut, Jessah poked her head out from under the blankets. Her friend's fallen countenance gave clear indication that things had not gone well. Quickly jumping out of bed, she hurried to Yona's side so they could talk in relative privacy.

"What's wrong?" she whispered.

"Miss Moselle has informed me that I have been selected to help Ms. Bina around her house. I am to move in with her as a housemaid doing all the chores and duties she needs done," Yona explained dejectedly. "All I know is that she is old and needs my help."

This new information took Jessah by surprise. She had clearly been flooded with peace when conferring with Elemet regarding Yona. Though she did not understand all that was going on, she remained confident things would still turn out fine. All she could do was encourage her friend to remain positive.

"But Yona, that is wonderful! Think of how much more freedom you will have! Maybe Ms. Bina is really nice and will give you time for yourself as well. Maybe she will even be like real family to you! Wouldn't that be amazing?"

"Maybe," she conceded, "but what about our friendship? I won't be able to see you every day like we are used to."

"Oh, don't you worry! You know I have my ways of getting around when I need to. We will always be friends. You can be sure of that! So, let's just wait and see how all this works out. I have a feeling it will be just fine. Ok?"

Yona had to agree. She really didn't know a lot about Ms. Bina and it could possibly be a great blessing to her. Besides, what choice did she have? Once something was decided for the good of a village or the island, there was no more discussion permitted.

"How much time did Miss Moselle say you had before the move?"

"Maybe a couple of days," Yona replied, biting her lip a bit to hold back the tears. "You know, you are like a real sister to me. How will I possibly survive without you?"

Without commenting, Jessah wrapped her arms around her friend giving her a squeeze. The first bell clanged loudly throughout the facility during their hug indicating it was time for them to head to class. The other girls in the barren room began moving towards the door, so Jessah quickly whispered into Yona's ear informing her that she would soon be off on another adventure and would return around lunch time. Yona nodded in assent.

As the second bell rang out, all the girls filed out to stand in their appropriate lines. Miss Moselle appeared right on cue and proceeded to lead the girls to their afternoon classes. Everyone followed in single file, except for Jessah. She headed in a completely different direction. Yona only briefly glanced back in time to see her friend disappear around the corner.

Once safely outside the confines of Camp Shabelle, Jessah moved freely between the trees, though attentive to assure no one was watching her. This was a new route for her, not like the visits to see Miss Haddie. However, she did have a good distance to walk, so Jessah set her pace at a brisk walk while heading towards the village of Kieran.

Something was definitely going on.

Chapter Nine

WORDS, WORDS, WORDS

As Shoshanna pushed her way through the branches and brush, she couldn't seem to stop the tears that would occasionally drip down her face as she progressed towards the homestead. She was certain she would receive a stern correction, which she deserved, from the dear old woman she had grown to love in just a brief period of time.

Calling herself every possible derogatory name she could think of throughout her journey, Shoshanna chided herself harshly for such carelessness. Her mind continually replayed visions of Galen being led away to prison. In addition to this disturbing event were her concerns of possible rejection by her beloved teacher and mentor. And all this happened because she had simply taken liberties in regards to her directions given by Miss Haddie.

"I wouldn't be surprised if she banned me from ever coming to see her again," she muttered to herself, "and I wouldn't blame her in the least! How could I have been so dumb?"

And poor Galen! What could be happening to him in that horrible prison? she wondered. They could be beating him or even torturing him for all she knew. Tears ran down her cheeks again as she thought about the trauma Galen's parents must have experienced while watching their son be handcuffed and led away.

The sorrow and grief eventually moved her to consider the cold-hearted men who arrested Galen. How could they simply arrest a man without any consideration of whether there was truth behind the accusations or not?

"Those thugs! Why can't they just leave us be so we can live our lives without their interference?" she angrily mumbled to herself.

Recalling how Galen's arrest was a result of his non-compliance to the ways of their society, she suddenly wondered if her own choices might someday affect her father as well. Would he be forced at some point to watch his own daughter be led away in handcuffs? She couldn't bear that thought!

By the time she arrived at the homestead, her thoughts and emotions were in a jumbled mess! Miss Haddie was quick to meet her at the door and escorted her in as Shoshanna attempted to explain everything that had occurred from the last time they had seen each other. Sitting patiently, the older woman listened allowing Shoshanna to express all that had been bottled up inside during her journey.

When she finished, Shoshanna then braced herself for the rebuke she knew she deserved. Instead, Miss Haddie simply handed her a handkerchief for her to wipe away her tears and walked over to the stove to heat up some water.

"Would you like some tea, my dear?" she called out over her shoulder.

"Uh, I-I guess. I am pretty thirsty and dry. Yes, thank you."

Stunned by her calmness, Shoshanna watched her at the stove as she poured the hot water into the cups. Certainly when she returned, she would launch into the inevitable scolding. However, Miss Haddie simply came back with two cups of tea in hand and set them carefully on the table before them.

Pulling up a chair to sit down, Miss Haddie began. "My dear, I am not going to scold you for choosing to delay the delivery of the message to Galen. I am certain that you have already suffered enough anguish over this poor decision."

Tears of relief flowed down her face once again as she strove to focus on what else her teacher had to say about the matter.

"Rather than agonizing any further, let's look at what can be learned from this incident. Tell me, what has this experience taught you?"

Picking up the handkerchief again to wipe her face, Shoshanna took a moment to reconsider the whole affair from a new light.

"Well," she began slowly, "I learned that it is very important to listen to instructions and follow them exactly though I may not fully understand why it must be done that way."

"Good! Now what else?"

"I realized that decisions I make on my own may profoundly impact others in a very negative way," she admitted. This disclosure reminded her of the recipient most impacted by her poor choices. "And what about poor Galen? Because of me he is sitting in a prison going through who knows what…and it is all my fault!"

Once again, tears began rolling down her cheeks.

"Let's not worry too much about Galen right now," Miss Haddie consoled her. "You forget he has uncommon light and will be protected through all this as he listens to Elemet for himself. Now, one more important matter you must consider. What was the thing most motivating you to delay delivering the message to Galen?"

Taking a deep breath, the young woman examined her own heart in the matter.

"I guess I was feeling a little tired and really didn't want to begin a whole new journey after arriving at my home."

"Exactly," she said, applauded her clarity. "You were focusing on what was comfortable and most convenient for you rather than concentrating on the mission you had been given. That is where so many of us stumble and fall in the beginning of our walk with Elemet."

Shoshanna was taken back a bit by this.

"Do you mean that you have stumbled in this area as well?" she asked incredulously.

"Oh yes, dear! And probably more than one time, especially in the beginning."

"Not you! I can't imagine you ever failing in anything."

"Well, let me assure you, I also had to be trained to listen carefully and follow directions exactly. This is a very important and valuable lesson you have learned, one that will serve you well in the days ahead."

Shoshanna was already beginning to feel better about herself, though she still had many questions.

"Now there is something very important that we must attend to," Miss Haddie continued. "As you were traveling here, did you hear the voice of the darkness telling you terrible things about yourself?"

"Well, I don't know if it was the voice of darkness, but I did call myself a number of names, kicking myself for how foolish I had been. What I said about myself was true, though."

"If you were hearing and repeating those horrible things about yourself, then you certainly did hear the voice of darkness. Those are the things darkness says about you, but that is not the way Elemet feels about you. The very essence of Elemet is love, life and encouragement, not destructive words that leave you feeling worthless."

Seeing her confusion in this new revelation, Miss Haddie explained how each person was created in the beginning by the source of all light and was even doted upon by Elemet himself. Within each child was placed amazing treasures and gifts from him.

With this seed of light within them, each person also carried the same attributes as the light, but were given the ability to choose whether or not they would walk and speak in agreement with the truth or not. Once born into the world they lived in, darkness immediately set at work to destroy the light and distort every gift and treasure given to them.

"But how does darkness destroy light and distort gifts?"

"It first starts in your mind, where words of death and destruction are deposited. If we become convinced these words are true and then speak them out loud, it won't be long before those words of death and destruction will dictate and control how we live our lives," Miss Haddie continued.

"You see, we carry within us the ability to agree with darkness, thereby empowering it in our lives, or we can agree with the truth which eventually dispels the darkness around us."

"And what about the treasures and gifts placed within us? How do we access them?" Shoshanna asked.

"It's really not a matter of accessing them, but rather training ourselves to hear the right voice and respond. As we speak in agreement with Elemet, we also learn to follow the light as directed and with that discover new abilities and authority within. With practice, we will be able to properly handle and use that which is rightfully ours."

"Each person you meet is either walking in agreement with truth, walking in agreement with darkness, or has chosen to live in a powerless state with a mixture of the two. This is where some truth and some darkness have blended together in a person's mind. This grey state leaves them with little ability to resist or even discern darkness, so it is quite easy for them to fall into traps leading to their own destruction."

Distraught with the idea that darkness might be able to deceive and destroy her own life as well as the lives of others, Shoshanna questioned her further. "But what can people do if they recognized their need for more truth and light?"

"We are back to the power of their own words and choices. All one has to do is first acknowledge their need for truth and then ask Elemet for his help. We ask for his light, his love and his wisdom which allows us to live exactly as we were designed to be. We can be free of darkness and filled with the joy of discovery as we learn who we are and what we are capable of."

"That is exactly what I want!" she declared. "Can you help me with this?"

"Certainly, child. But understand you are new in learning the distinction of voices and gaining greater clarity all the time. However, there still may be occasions when things may appear unclear to you at first. That's when you need to stop and rest your mind in the peace and love of Elemet. Talk to him and ask for what you need. You will soon come to hear and recognize his voice very well. He is the source of our confidence and the discovery of more than either of us could ever conceive."

Supper was long past by the time Shoshanna arrived back at her home. Even as the sun was growing dimmer behind the horizon, Shoshanna was beaming with joy as she stepped into her home. Though she felt delight through and through, Oren, her father was not quite as pleased. The late hour of her return upset and worried him. Realizing she would need help in dealing with this situation, the young woman took a moment to rest her mind in this new love of Elemet and before she even had time to ask, the wisdom she needed was there.

Chapter Ten

FREEDOM EVEN IN "SECURITY"

Galen sat dejectedly staring at the dense stone walls surrounding him in his small cell. The cell contained two simple wooden planked beds on each side, and there was a single window with thick metal bars imbedded into the bulwark. His current circumstances, at first glance, did not appear to be good in any way, and he was having a difficult time trying to cope with his emotions.

He glanced from wall to wall estimating it to be maybe eight feet across and eight feet wide. Not much space to move around in, for sure. His mind was still spinning at how quickly his freedom had been taken from him. However, what he found most disturbing was the idea that Tanzi, his best friend's mother, had been the one to viciously accuse him of resisting the "perfect" system devised by the village elders to "protect and maintain" their fragile existence on Kumani. He had suspected she had listened to his conversation with Roany. And now it was obvious: she had.

In addition to this, Galen's heart was greatly troubled for Roany. He recalled how they had begun the journey of discovering freedom together as friends. They had even discussed going to the smoking mountains located in the center of the island to see if they could determine whether the smoke was a real threat or not. Rumors of a possible volcanic eruption had circulated throughout the villages for years. They both wondered if this was actually the case or if something else was at play. But now, their curiosity appeared as a fading dream while Galen sat physically imprisoned and Roany lived imprisoned in his mind, with neither of them seeing a way out at the moment.

Galen was also mystified as to why he had not been forewarned by either the light or the voice of Elemet prior to his arrest. In the past, he had always received a warning when trouble was headed in his direction, but not this time. He considered the idea that maybe a greater purpose lay behind his arrest. Only time would tell. And until then, there was nothing he could do.

He hadn't spent much time slouched against the wall before a young, smiling face appeared in his window.

"Jessah! What in the world are you doing? And how did you get up to this second floor window?"

Jessah laughed at his surprised expression. "Didn't you notice this lovely vine growing up the side of the wall? Climbing up it was easy!"

"What?" Galen moved over to the window, and stepping up on the edge of his bed, he was able to peer down at the wall. There was indeed a thick vine with outstretched branches hugging the stone-walled bulwark allowing little Jessah to scamper up its branches like a squirrel.

"Okay. I see you have great climbing abilities. Very impressive. However, this is a very dangerous place. You shouldn't be here at all!"

"Well, I don't think it is too dangerous if Elemet has sent me here," she responded, still smiling. "I have a message and some instructions for you."

"Really! I wondered what he had in mind," Galen responded.

"Elemet says that you will be here for a little while longer, but not to worry. There is someone he wants you to speak with; another prisoner. After that, you will be able to walk out. When you are free, you are to head towards the Eagles' Nest. He will give you more details later."

"Walk out of here? I wonder how that could happen."

"I don't know exactly," she admitted, "but you do remember that I walk out of Camp Shabelle all the time."

"That's true!" he conceded. "Well then, I guess I better make myself comfortable for a while until it is time for my walkabout."

Just at that moment, a heavy-stepping guard began moving down the corridor towards Galen's cell. The jingle of his heavy keys grew louder as he approached.

"Oh, I better go now. Bye!"

Galen quickly sat down on his hard wooden bed as the guard struggled with the key for a moment while attempting to unlock the cell door. Finally the deadbolt released and the heavy, iron-bound door groaned as it swung open.

Without a spoken word, the guard roughly pushed in a second man through the doorway before pulling the door closed behind him. Once again, the key turned and the deadbolt was locked in place leaving the two men blankly staring at each other for a moment. After sizing up his situation, the new inmate sauntered over to his bed dropping down heavily upon it.

Things were already becoming clearer in Galen's mind. He just needed to speak with this goliath of a man, tell him about Elemet, and then Galen would be able to walk out of here. Easy!

After a time of deafening silence, the man finally turned his head towards Galen. He was obviously upset with how things had played out in his life and was not in a particularly friendly mood. His thick auburn curls upon his head, shook as he as he spoke, while glaring at his new cellmate.

"I'm Uri," he announced, "and I don't intend to put up with anything that crosses me!"

"Ok, Uri. Good to know. I'm Galen," he said extending out his hand in friendship.

Uri stared at Galen's hand for a moment, but did not respond. Instead, he angrily turned his head straight ahead, staring at the wall before him. He had no intention of responding.

Galen's hand dropped to his side. This is not going to be easy, he thought to himself. Taking a breath and closing his eyes, he decided it was time to refocus and get some clarity on his new "assignment."

Chapter Eleven

A PERFECT PLAN

By the following morning, Shoshanna's father had calmed down from the previous night's escapade and was back to his normal self. Her carefully worded explanation of the preparation process she was undergoing with Miss Haddie helped him calm down. With much effort on Shoshanna's part, Oren eventually understood the need for the occasional extended sessions with "the eagle lady." as Shoshanna referred to her.

Shoshanna allowed her father to watch as she prepared food for some prisoners in the nearby village of Kieran. Apparently, the eagle lady had some friends there who needed help in bringing meals to the inmates. At least that is what Shoshanna told her father.

Content to see his daughter practicing her cooking skills at home, Oren finally left for his butcher shop while Shoshanna quickly finished putting together the meal. Shortly afterwards, she rushed out the door heading for Kieran. She was extremely anxious to see what had become of Galen.

After her first trip to Kieran being entirely led by the light before her, Shoshanna was much more confident in her travels. Across her arm, she carried the same basket she had used to deliver the apple pie to her father only days ago.

As she walked, there were still occasions where she briefly entertained thoughts of maybe taking a short detour before going to the prison so she could apologize to Galen's parents for her mistake. However, Miss Haddie had warned her about this. They would not understand any of what was actually happening and it would just aggravate the problem. Besides, this was now her second opportunity to follow directions exactly without changing or altering them in any way. Shoshanna was determined to execute her instructions perfectly this time.

It was nearly midday by the time Shoshanna arrived at the prison door donning a hooded cape. The hood covered parts of her face in hopes it would help mask her identity to some degree. Stepping up to the guard, she informed him that she had been asked to bring a meal to one of the prisoners inside rather than Cherith, who had suddenly become ill. The guard lifted the cloth off the basket to insure only food was being taken in and then stepped aside allowing her entry.

Shoshanna entered the darkened building where only a few lanterns were lit inside revealing the corridors leading off in several directions. Immediately in front of her was a steep spiral staircase going up to the next floor. As she had learned, Shoshanna took a moment to settle herself with eyes closed. As soon as she opened her eyes, the light flickered before her indicating she was to climb up the stairway to the second floor of the building.

By the time she reached the top of the stairs, she was led to go right and began moving slowly down the darkened hall. Heavily locked and bolted doors lined both sides of the corridor. Above each door a number was etched into the wood giving the only indication as to where a particular prisoner might be. As she moved down the hallway, door by door, the wooden beams creaked beneath her. She heard some muffled movements behind several of the entrances, but she was only interested in one in particular.

The guiding light she followed suddenly stopped in front of one door. Taking note of the number, she boldly walked down to the guard stationed on the other end of the hallway and asked if she could bring the planned meal to the prisoner behind door 24. Nodding, the guard walked to the door and opened it, allowing Shoshanna to bring in the food basket.

She was a bit surprised to see a second prisoner in the small room with Galen, especially one of his size. She managed to maintain her composure before the guard acting as though this was business as usual. Galen stood up before them allowing Shoshanna to walk over and set the basket on his bed.

Turning to the guard, she asked if she could have a moment to show the prisoners the food she had prepared. Clearly uninterested in the whole event, the guard just muttered something under his breath and stepped back away from the door.

Sitting down on the bed, Shoshanna began unpacking the basket for the prisoners. Galen stood close by pretending to inspect the food as she slowly lifted out each item, one by one.

"Oh Galen," she whispered. "I am so sorry all this happened. I was supposed to deliver a warning to you from Miss Haddie two days ago. Instead I stayed home that night and came yesterday morning just as you were being arrested."

Galen nodded and gave her a half-smile of acknowledgement.

She could feel tears beginning to well up again as she peered into his eyes. Trying to avoid any undo emotion, she quickly turned her attention back to the food she had brought. One by one, she pulled out cinnamon biscuits, fruit, and a meat pie for them to enjoy.

"Well, thank you, miss. This all looks so wonderful," Galen stated while examining one of the apples. Then, lowering his voice, he whispered that Jessah had come by and he had been given a new assignment.

Nodding his head briefly in the direction of his cellmate, Shoshanna glanced over at the huge man staring attentively at both the food and the young woman delivering their meal. She smiled. Uri did not return the smile. Glancing back at Galen with a puzzled look, he just shrugged his shoulders and smiled, shaking his head.

As Shoshanna reached for the handle of the basket preparing to leave, Galen put his hand on top of hers and gave it a squeeze.

"Thank you," he said, but his eyes said much more.

Walking her to the door, Galen leaned close to her ear and whispered, "Don't worry. I won't be here too long."

Shoshanna smiled in relief and then called the guard letting him know she was done. Gruffly, he scuffled over to the door locking it behind her as she left. With the empty basket on her arm, she headed back down the hallway to the staircase leading down and then out of the prison.

Meanwhile, back in the cell, Uri never moved from his bed, but with squinted eyes, continued staring at Galen. He was obviously very suspicious.

Galen smiled once again attempting to connect with his cellmate.

"Would you like an apple?" he asked while holding out the fruit in front of him.

Uri cautiously eyed the fruit and Galen for a moment, before grabbing the apple. As he chomped into the fruit, his countenance seemed to soften a bit.

Maybe this is going to be okay, he thought to himself as he settled down on his bed to also enjoy the food.

After eating in silence for some time, Uri suddenly spoke.

"So, was that your wife?" he asked without even looking up from the biscuit he held in front of him. Stunned, Galen looked over at him wondering why he would ask such a question.

"No, she was just a friend," he replied.

"Too bad. She's quite a looker, and someone's going to be snatching her up pretty quick here for sure."

Galen gazed at him for a moment, speculating as to why Uri would assume she was his wife, and secondly, why he thought someone would be "snatching her up" so quickly. That idea actually bothered him a bit.

With things set up on Kumani as they were, he wasn't even sure how he would go about getting himself a wife. To be honest, he had been so distracted by all the hullabaloo and control issues of the village elders, the last thing on his mind was a wife. All of that would have to wait for another time. First, he needed to focus on getting out of this cell and then making his way towards the Eagles' Nest. That was enough for now.

Try as he might to dismiss Uri's words, he had to admit there was some attraction to Shoshanna. Her courage and humility in confessing her mistake caught his attention. And she was a "looker" as Uri said. Too bad things weren't different on Kumani, he thought. He actually wouldn't mind at all if Shoshanna and he could be together. However, with him now labeled as a convicted dissenter, there was little hope that he would have any kind of "normal" life. He had no idea what the Eagles' Nest was like and only hoped things would be very different there.

With a full stomach and many things to consider, Galen made himself as comfortable as could be expected on such a hard bed and shut his eyes. He thought again about his move to the Eagles' Nest and what impact that might have on his parents. He knew they were already worried about him and the direction of his life.

Realizing his arrest would cause them to worry about him, he only hoped that someone would be able to bring them some degree of comfort. At that moment, they had no idea what was going on and if they would ever see their son again. Without question, he knew their own fears would prevent them from trying to see him lest they be considered a part of the dissenters themselves.

It's just like Miss Haddie explained, he told himself. Fear and self-preservation keep many powerless against darkness.

It was obvious that his parents did not fully subscribe to all that was being forced upon the people of Kumani, but at the same time, their own fears kept them enslaved. Living under the control of darkness was no life at all. Yes, he would rather live in agreement with the truth of Elemet and be imprisoned than live imprisoned by his own fears wherever he was.

With his eyes shut, he could feel sleep coming upon him. As there was nothing more he could do at the moment, he repositioning himself and prepared to take a nap. It didn't take long for his mind to drift asleep, but even as he was sleeping, the light was at work in him and around him.

Chapter Twelve

A CHANGE OF PLANS

Jessah giggled as she recalled Galen's expression when she showed her face outside the prison bars of his cell. It almost felt like a dream, how easily she had scaled the prison wall. Elemet had brilliantly planned for a vine to grow in that exact location allowing her to reach window she needed. Joy washed over her each time she accomplished what she had been asked to do and sometimes that joy was hard to explain. She so loved bringing hope and encouragement to others!

Though only ten, or nearly ten, Jessah had learned very quickly about Elemet, his light and the ways of the eagle, as they called it. With the haze hanging over the villages of Kumani, she had never actually seen an eagle before, however, Miss Haddie had told her wonderful stories about the eagles. She told Jessah how eagles at one time could be seen far above the clouds soaring effortlessly in the winds. From their high vantage point these eagles were able to see everything below clearly.

"One day, I will see eagles for myself," Jessah declared aloud to squirrels scampering up the sides of the trees around her, "and then I will learn to soar high above the haze and even the mountains as I see Kumani and Camp Shabelle far below me!"

She beamed as she thought about it.

Now that her morning "errand" was complete, she only had a short distance left before arriving back at Camp Shabelle. Soon she would re-enter the gate, come back inside, and rejoin her group just as it had always happened in the past. As she slipped back inside the training center, however, she noticed a difference in the atmosphere. That tension made her feel a little uncomfortable.

Using greater caution than normal, she moved down the familiar darkened hallway. She stopped several times to listen for further instructions, but heard nothing. Suddenly she saw the light leading in a different direction than what she was used to. Without hesitation, she followed it to an obscure window in the corner of Miss Moselle's office. Slowly moving her head upward, she saw Yona standing in her office with her head dropped listening to Miss Moselle detail what had been recently decided about her future.

"As you know, Camp Shabelle was established as training facility for young children who are orphans. With the increase of orphans coming into our facility from around the island and our limited space, we have decided that once a child reaches the age of twelve, they will be immediately shipped off to begin their apprenticeship training working in the areas necessary for their own usefulness in society."

"I told you earlier today that it would be a couple of days before you were to move in with Ms. Bina," Miss Moselle continued, "however, I have just been informed that there is a new group of orphans being brought to us shortly, and we simply must make room for the new arrivals. Therefore, you will pack your bags and any belongings immediately as are all the other twelve-year-olds in this facility. You will be moving in with Ms. Bina immediately as her new housemaid. Understand?"

Yona was silent for a moment, then did the unspeakable. "But Miss Moselle, I am not yet twelve years old. There is still a couple months before my next birthday. Couldn't I wait just a little longer before starting with Ms. Bina?"

Miss Moselle's eyes widened as she slowly raised her head to look upon the child who dared question her decisions in any matter. She stared at the nearly twelve-year-old, still aghast at her nerve to say anything. Silently, she considered what her response might be.

No one EVER challenged Miss Moselle.

"Young lady, you have just lost the privilege of collecting your things before leaving," she fumed. "Your clothes will be gathered for you and sent over to Ms. Bina's home. All personal belongings will be destroyed. Your bed is needed for the incoming orphans. It is time for you to head to the entryway where you will be taken to Ms. Bina's house immediately. Mr. Tobin will escort you there. Go now!"

Tears were already streaming down Yona's face as Mr. Tobin was summoned to accompany her to the front door where she would immediately be transported to the house.

Jessah now knew why she had been led to the office instead of joining her usual group.

Racing back to their dorm, Jessah quickly gathered what few treasured possessions Yona had in their room and safely hid them among her own belongings. The timing was perfect, of course. Just as she had left the room, she spotted Miss Moselle's staff members heading in to gather up her friend's clothing, change the bedding, and dispose of any personal items left behind. Fortunately, there was nothing personal that they could find and in short order had all of Yona's clothing stuffed in a bag which was taken to her as she waited at the front door to be escorted to her new home.

Without any further incidents, Jessah was quietly able to join the other girls in her group as they headed towards the mess hall where lunch was to be served. Though the food seemed almost edible, Jessah has lost her appetite as she thought about poor Yona being taken to a strange home to be put to work as nothing more than a household servant.

She dabbled at her food while imagining the distress her friend must be feeling regarding the loss of the few reminders Yona had of her parents. Though Jessah had rescued her treasures, it would be a little time before she could return them to her friend. With this new group of girls coming in, it would require a period of careful observation for her to acquire new wisdom on when to escape and return unseen by the newcomers.

Her heart was already beginning to feel weighed down by the departure of her closest friend from Camp Shabelle. The loss of Yona much sooner than expected was definitely a huge blow. Her stomach twisted in knots as she thought about it. The more she considered the changes, the worse she felt. The bliss and freedom she had been walking in earlier that day seemed to vanish as the haze pressed in all around her.

Quickly recognizing the loss of her own peace and joy, Jessah knew it was time to have a talk with Elemet. She was desperate to get settled back into the light and love which had always dispelled the darkness in her life, a darkness which was attempting to creep in at that very moment.

Chapter Thirteen

SHOSHANNA'S PLEA

"**B**ut you should have seen their faces! His parents must be absolutely sick with worry about their son," Shoshanna coaxed. "Can't you put yourself in their place for a moment? We have to do something!"

Miss Haddie studied Shoshanna's face while silently asking for wisdom in this matter. Shoshanna's passionate plea on their behalves was not going to subside, that was obvious. She took another sip of her tea before responding to the young woman.

"Okay. I'm feeling a release to have you deliver another gift from me to help encourage them during this time. However, I must caution you not to say too much. Say only what I give you to say on my behalf. You mustn't even let on how well you know Galen. Is that understood?"

"Yes ma'am," she responded excitedly. "I'll only say what you want me to and do exactly as you direct. Thank you for doing this!"

"Remember, I am only passing on to you the wisdom I am being given. Elemet is the one responding to your request," Miss Haddie said while beginning to gather supplies for Shoshanna to deliver to Galen's parents. They both knew there was a risk involved with this mission of mercy, but Shoshanna was insistent that they try.

The afternoon sun was already moving towards the horizon by the time Shoshanna approached the home of Eber and Giza, Galen's parents. As she drew closer, she suddenly had flashbacks of that terrible moment when she saw the enforcers approaching the house, pounding on the door, and demanding Galen. She still felt heartsick about the whole affair, but at least now she was able to bring a little comfort to his parents.

She looked down at the new basket she had been given carrying tea, some fresh cut flowers, and, of course, an apple pie straight from the kitchen of Miss Haddie. Realizing that they would press her for more information about their son, she silently asked for both wisdom and strength not to reveal all that she knew. She needed to deliver the message from Miss Haddie and reveal no more.

"I can do this," she told herself. Taking one last breath of courage, she boldly strolled across the meadow where the house was situated. Arriving at their front door, she decided to lightly knock while calling out so as not to alarm his parents any further.

"Hello? Is anybody home?" she asked. After waiting for a moment, she noticed the door slowly cracking open only allowing the residents a glimpse of their visitor. Shoshanna put her face close to the door so they could clearly see her.

"Hi! I'm Shoshanna, a friend of Miss Haddie." she said smiling, "She asked me to deliver a few things to you on her behalf."

The door quickly shut.

She could hear some discussion between the couple as they whispered back and forth. Finally, the door swung open. Giza stood in the forefront with her white apron tied around her waist and her loosely fitting dress nearly touching the floor. Her brown hair was pulled back tightly in a bun with streaks of gray revealing her obvious maturity. Loose curly strands framed her worn face as she attempted to smile at their visitor. Eber stood at a distance behind his wife, scowling. He was obviously not convinced that Shoshanna should be allowed into their home at all.

Sensing their suspicions, Shoshanna attempted to make them feel as comfortable as possible. "Oh, I hope I am not disturbing you," she assured them. "I won't stay long. I just wanted to drop off a few gifts from Miss Haddie. She told me it has been a while since she sent you some of her tea and wanted to make sure you were adequately supplied."

At that comment, the silvery haired man rolled his eyes and walked away from the door. Giza, not wanting to appear ungrateful, invited Shoshanna in encouraging her to sit at the table for a cup of tea herself. Once inside, Shoshanna brought out not only the delicious tea, but also the flowers and the mouth-watering apple pie which was set aside for later.

Greatly touched by her kindness, Giza relaxed some as she prepared tea for the two of them to enjoy. Once the tea was properly steeped and the brightly colored bouquet was placed in a vase in the center of the table, Giza brought the warm spicy tea for the two of them to enjoy.

"So, my dear, how did you come to know Miss Haddie?" she asked curious about her connection to this mystery woman.

Recalling all the instructions she had been given, Shoshanna smiled and as nonchalantly as she could muster up, she said, "Oh, I met her on one of my walks around the island. She was so sweet and kind, we quickly became friends. I go to see her every once in a while. On this last visit, she asked me to deliver these gifts to you, and I agreed."

Giza sipped on her tea a bit, obviously considering what to ask next. "So, where exactly does this Miss Haddie live? She has sent some gifts in the past through our son, Galen, and we would love to thank her in person sometime."

This was the question Miss Haddie had warned her about.

"Oh, is Galen your son? I believe I met him before. He seemed like a very nice man."

"Yes, Galen is our son. Unfortunately, he is not around right at the moment or I'm sure he would be happy to see you himself." Giza cleared her throat obviously trying not to think about recent events. "Would you be sure to send our thanks to Miss Haddie for this delicious tea, the flowers, and the pie she sent? That was very kind of her."

"Yes, Miss Haddie is very thoughtful like that," Shoshanna assured her.

Realizing that no more useful information would be coming from Shoshanna, Giza conceded to just enjoying the company of this sweet young lady. The two began chatting about other issues of life and suddenly Shoshanna found herself telling Giza all about her mother's untimely death. Giza's heart was deeply touched by her story and even found herself offering advice to this motherless daughter.

By the time their tea was gone, Shoshanna knew it was time for her to leave, so she stood and headed towards the door. Giza followed her, feeling saddened that her new, young friend had to leave.

"Will you come by to see me again sometime?" Giza asked hopefully.

"Of course! I would love to!"

"I hope your return visit would not be too long of a journey for you," Giza said. "I have enjoyed your company."

Shoshanna smiled realizing that she, too, had grown quite fond of this woman. "It's not too far at all," she assured her. Noticing that Eber was outside doing some work around their home, she decided it was time to deliver the final message from Miss Haddie.

"Before I leave, Miss Haddie asked me to let you know one more thing." Giza eyes lit up in hope as Shoshanna continued. "She asked me to tell you Galen is fine and will not be confined for long. She encourages you not to worry. She says there is a much bigger plan here at work."

Tears formed in her new friend's eyes with this new information. Shoshanna proceeded with her message.

"She also asked that you do not share this with anyone beyond your husband, for Galen's sake." Giza quickly nodded as the tears slipped out and ran down her worn face.

In the slim hope of maintaining her identity as only a messenger, Shoshanna added, "Miss Haddie wanted me to tell you that."

After delivering her message, Shoshanna looked deeply into this mother's eyes and then hugged her as if she was her own, greatly-missed mother.

"I will try to come back and visit you again, if I can," Shoshanna promised. Almost in a whisper, she added, "Don't give up hope."

Once again the two embraced before Shoshanna headed back towards her own home. Glancing over her shoulder to wave, she noticed Eber had joined Giza at the door. Even from a distance, she could see Giza excitedly explaining to her husband all that had been relayed. Shoshanna felt an explosion of joy and love washing over her as she realized she had accomplished what she had been sent to do.

Yes, there was nothing like following the light and obeying instructions as they are given, she decided. However, beyond that she recognized her own need for motherly attention. Elemet had mercifully arranged for this meeting. Miss Haddie might be her teacher, but Giza was much like the missing mother in her life.

While walking back to her father and their home, Shoshanna was suddenly reminded of her brief visit with Galen and the quick squeeze he had given her hand as he helped her pick up the basket. As she thought further about it, she felt a little stir of emotion she had not experienced before.

Not wanting to read more into a simple squeeze of the hand, she decided to dismiss the whole thing. She knew Galen would shortly be heading to the Eagles' Nest. All she cared about was that she was finally happy and feeling so content with this new way of living. There was definitely no going back for her at this point.

Chapter Fourteen

MAKING A WAY

When Galen finally awoke from his nap, he realized that he had slept through the remainder of the day and now it was very late in the evening, or possibly very early in the morning of the following day. He had no idea. Either way, he could hear Uri loudly snoring beside him and it was probably his cellmate's snoring that woke him up.

Getting up from his bed, he walked over to the barred window noticing the full orange-red moon attempting to shine down through the haze hanging over the prison. Its weakened glow fought to break through the stifling night air, much like he himself fought to bring clarity to those around him.

Though he knew there would eventually be a way of escape for him, the idea that village elders were deciding his fate, still bothered him. Anyone found in dissension to their "perfect plan" faced a real possibility of death. However, he also was aware of their need for healthy young men to do hard labor in remote locations around the island.

Because of his physical strength, he imagined they would select him for hard labor.

If it hadn't been for Jessah taking a great risk and delivering Elemet's message to him earlier, he might have had to face a very stark future indeed. Once again he looked down from his cell, still quite amazed that she had climbed up that vine just to inform him of what to expect.

Sitting back down on his bunk, he tried to clearly recall every detail of the message he had been given. He remembered that Elemet said he would not be behind bars for long. That was a relief! He recalled something about talking to a prisoner and then he would be able to walk out of here. Glancing over at the sleeping giant on the bunk next to him, he was actually a little relieved that Uri was unwilling to talk with him. Uri seemed like he would be a difficult person to get along with.

So how does one walk out of a locked and heavily guarded prison? And then I'm supposed to go to the Eagles' Nest, wherever that is, he mused. Sure! No problem at all.

As he sat pondering it all, he suddenly heard a clicking coming from the door of his cell. Walking over to the door, he gave it a slight yank and stood stunned as it pulled open in front of him.

"Well, I guess that is how it is done," he whispered to himself, half-laughing. Looking back behind him to assure Uri was still sleeping, he prepared to slip out the door. Just as he was getting ready to leave, he heard a stirring behind him.

"Where do you think you are going?"

Galen whipped around only to see Uri sitting upright and wide awake. He quickly realized that he wasn't going anywhere with Uri watching him intently.

"If you are thinking about leaving, you best consider bringing me along. I can be pretty loud if I choose to be and you wouldn't want that right now, would you?"

Galen had to smile. He was right. He couldn't possibly leave Uri behind to whatever fate the elders had planned for him.

"Well, if you want to come, you better get moving because I don't know how much time we have to get out of this building without being detected."

Uri was immediately up and standing right next to Galen. Looking upward at the massive man, Galen realized that he was nearly a full head taller than himself. Uri would be difficult to hide and even harder to blend into a crowd with his auburn hair standing out like a red flag on the top of his head. Galen wondered if getting him to move silently through the facility might be a little like a herding a bull. Definitely, a bit tricky indeed.

"By the way, how did you open this door anyway?" Uri inquired, still stunned that they were actually getting ready to escape.

"I just heard it unlock," Galen whispered back. "Now I need you to be as quiet as possible so we can get out of here. Okay?"

"Yeah, sure. I'll be quiet." Nodding back at him, Galen proceeded to push the door open very slowly, inches at a time. As soon as the door opened wide enough for them both to slip through, they moved out into the darkened hallway with Uri closing the door behind him. As soon as the door was closed, they heard the door lock behind them.

"I didn't do that!" Uri whispered to Galen.

"I know, I know," he responded. "Just follow me without saying anything else. Okay?" Uri nodded in assent. Galen only hoped Uri actually knew how to be quiet.

The two men silently moved down the corridor where they could hear a number of snoring men behind the locked doors. When they finally arrived at the spiral staircase with its massive guard station right next to the entrance, they hesitated for a moment wondering if anyone might be awake and alert at that hour.

Slowly they began their descent. Each stair creaked loudly as Uri stepped down one by one. Galen groaned silently as he led the way to whatever awaited them. They had obviously been assisted this far. More assistance would definitely be needed for their escape from the prison.

Arriving at the ground floor, Galen quickly glanced over at the guard station. The three guards snored loudly with their chairs leaning back against the wall. Silently, the two men moved passed them, but were faced with a heavily bolted door barricading their only exit.

They looked at each other, wondering what to do next. Looking back at the door, they saw that the bolts had already been slid aside for them, and all they had to do was open the door and walk out. Even though the door screeched as it opened, the guards continued sleeping. They exited into the moonlight haze closing the door behind them, and heard the bolt slide back into place.

Clearly puzzled, Uri looked at Galen again.

"I know. You didn't do that either. Come on. Let's get out of here," Galen responded before Uri even had a chance to comment. The two men moved quickly away from the village of Kieran to a safer location where they could debrief and slip away in opposite directions.

Before long they were surrounded by the foliage of the forest and able to breathe a little easier. It was at this point that Galen turned to Uri with his hand once again outstretched. This time, however, Uri grabbed his hand and shook it heartily, nearly yanking Galen's arm out of its socket.

"We made it out, for sure! Now what?" Uri asked.

"Well," Galen responded, "this is where we part ways, I suppose."

Smiling broadly, he replied assertively, "Not on your life! After what I saw tonight, I am not about to walk away. Whatever all this is, I want to know more, and you're the one to tell me."

Remembering that Uri was not much for people crossing him, Galen took a breath and wisely decided there really was no safe way to tell this man "no."

"Well, okay then. I guess I can tell you what I know as we head towards our next destination."

"Okay, so start talking. I'm listening."

The two men starting walking in the night air with a full moon lighting the way, while Galen began explaining the truth and essence of real freedom to a man hungry for more.

Chapter Fifteen

WHAT ARE YOU DOING?

The moment finally came when Jessah was excused from the table and able to rush back to the room where she threw herself on the lower bunk and pulled the covers over her head. The sadness over the loss of her friend Yona was almost more than she could bear. An involuntary sob erupted from her as tears ran down her face in her only place of solitude in Camp Shabelle.

It was a little while before she was able to quiet her emotions and turn her attention back to hearing Elemet's voice. As she started talking with him, her first words were filled with self-pity and grief as she described her loneliness. With Yona leaving, she would now have to endure all the trials of Camp Shabelle by herself. It just didn't seem fair!

Elemet allowed her to unload all she was feeling and thinking before he responded to her.

"My child, who are you are focusing on at the moment?"

This surprised her a bit. "I'm telling you how I feel." There was no response, so she knew she didn't really answer his question. She took a moment to reconsider things. "I guess I am focusing on myself right now."

"Exactly. And when you first met me, what were you focusing on during that time as well?

Jessah stopped for a moment to recall the time several years back when her own parents had been killed in a terrible accident in the woods. The grief from that nearly overwhelmed her causing her to despair of life itself, until Elemet came in and revealed his great love and compassion for her. It was his love that healed her broken heart and gave her a new purpose for life on the island. All of a sudden, she began to understand.

"I was focusing on me and my loss," she admitted. "Then you came in, flooded me with your love, and showed me the wonderful life you had planned for me."

"How did you feel after I revealed myself to you?" He asked.

"I felt loved by you. I was filled with joy and peace."

"Has anything changed in my love for you?"

"No," she conceded.

"So, what are you doing?"

"I'm focusing on me instead of looking to you."

Though she couldn't see him with her eyes, she could sense his smile. Suddenly she realized how much he wanted free her from all that was robbing her joy. He wanted her remaining in peace even in the midst of difficult circumstances. Immediately, her attention was drawn away to his glorious love and beauty that surrounded her entire being. Her soul was opened up like a book, where all the pain and fear of loss was revealed and then was washed away by the glories of his realm. Once she was free, he spoke again to the child.

"Would you like to go flying with me?" he asked.

"What? Really?"

"Oh yes! Let's go flying this evening when you go to bed."

Jessah's heart filled with such inexpressible joy that she could hardly contain herself. When she threw the covers off herself and arose from her bunk, she was like a new person. The glow of her encounter was still upon her as stood to join the other girls beginning to assemble at the door. The second bell had rung indicating it was now time for all of them to be led to their classes and training.

As the girls stood next to her, they were inexplicably drawn to the joyful radiance reflecting off her face. One young girl leaned close to her asking about the change in her appearance. Jessah responded very simply with a huge smile.

"I'm going flying tonight."

Stunned by her answer, she was more puzzled than before but had no opportunity to ask any further questions. Miss Moselle appeared to escort them to their afternoon classes. Silently, they all lined up to follow the director, but even as they walked, the other girls kept glancing back at Jessah. Something had definitely changed in her!

The afternoon passed very quickly for Jessah as all she could think about was flying with Elemet. By the time supper was finished, she could hardly keep herself from running once again to her bunk where she knew a new encounter awaited her. When she returned back to her room, she quickly got ready for bed and then jumped in covering her face with a well-worn blanket each child was provided at Camp Shabelle.

It didn't take long for her to become quiet before Elemet. As she thought about the one who had always loved her, things began to slowly come into focus in her mind even as she drifted into sleep.

In her mind's eye, she saw the one who had created all things standing before her with a flowing white robe, eyes of fire, and prisms of light dancing around his radiant face. It was almost too bright for her to look at him, but eventually his brilliance dimmed to some degree so she could gaze upon him with greater ease.

Jessah had a hard time looking at anything else but him, however, she did notice something moving behind him. Noticing her curiosity, Elemet stepped aside allowing her to see what appeared to be a huge golden eagle gently flapping its outspread wings in excited expectation.

"Didn't you say you wanted to see the eagles for yourself and go soaring above Kumani and Camp Shabelle?" he asked her.

Jessah could hardly speak as she walked beside Elemet moving toward the great eagle. The massive bird looked upon her with great interest as she approached and placed her hand upon its gold-tinted feathers. His large eyes followed her as she walked around the bird, taking note of its sharp talons, with yellow, brown and white feathers all over its body. After a thorough examination of the amazing bird, she looked up to Elemet in awe.

"He is beautiful," she declared. "You have made him so lovely!"

Smiling Elemet replied, "Would you like to go flying now?"

Nodding, Jessah was overcome with joy and wonder as Elemet lifted her up upon the massive creature and then climbed up behind her. Within a few short seconds, the eagle flapped its wings and mounted up with ease into the sky. Breathlessly exhilarated with the wind brushing past her face, Jessah watched as they pushed through the clouds and burst into the clear blue heavens encircling the massive island that lay below them.

Though there was much cloud cover and haze over the island, with one sweep of his hand, Elemet cleared the skies below allowing Jessah to have an unobstructed view over the place she called home. It was not necessary to say much as the land was laid out before her with names and places clearly labeled as on a map. She carefully studied the land focusing on where things were in relationship to the other locations she was familiar with.

One new place she noticed was the Eagles' Nest. The place was massive, much larger than she had imagined and in a region she had never seen before. Houses, buildings, and large gardens of every type were scattered throughout the site. Magnificent cascading waterfalls pouring into one wide river which bordered the remaining sides of the region. One great bridge allowed entrance into this land.

While still enthralled with her aerial view of things, she noticed that the eagle had already begun its descent back to the hilltop where she had met Elemet. Turning backwards, she realized that Elemet was no longer sitting behind her. She was riding alone upon the great bird's back.

Just as they were preparing to fly through the clouds back to the land below, she happened to glance out upon the horizon and noticed something that looked very much like another island in the distance. Quickly the clouds surrounded them again and she lost sight of it, making her wonder if she had actually seen the island or not.

When they landed, Jessah slid off the eagle's back and slowly approached its sharp beak. She knew if he wanted to, he could easily injure her with one bite, but there was no fear in her heart, knowing this eagle was now her friend. Gently, she stroked the feathers around his head in appreciation for the wonderful ride he had given her.

In response to her gentle caress, the eagle bowed his head allowing her to hug the creature even as one of his large wings came around, wrapping the child in an embrace as well. Once their tender moment was over, the child backed off and began walking down the hill hoping the trail she was following would lead her back to Camp Shabelle.

Suddenly, her eyes opened and Jessah was back in her bunk with nothing but the worn, flimsy blanket once again covering her body. Though her body felt the chill of the dorm room, her heart was full and overflowing with the love and thrilling experience Elemet had granted her that night. Though it might have been nothing more than a wonderful dream, the experience was so vivid in her mind that she could recall every detail of their amazing flight.

She would never forget it!

As she turned on her side to find a warmer and more comfortable position in which to sleep, she felt something unusual underneath her arm. Reaching with her hand to grab the object, she suddenly realized it was a feather: A golden feather from the massive eagle itself! Discovering the feather just added to the overflowing joy she now felt. Carefully she placed it under her pillow and fell back asleep in great peace.

Chapter Sixteen

TIME CUT SHORT

Her father was unusually quiet during supper that night. His solemn face and furrowed eyebrows troubled her. Oren roughly chewed his food before swallowing as if trying to fill his stomach as quickly as possible. Shoshanna studied him between bites until she could stand no more.

"Father, what is going on with you this evening?"

Shaking his head, he could barely look her in the eyes. "I'm trying to figure out how to tell you something."

"Well, why don't you just say what you need to tell me?" she asked wondering what could be worse than the news he had already given her. The thought of her name on the list of eligible young women for the village elders to rummage through was troubling enough.

Taking a breath, Oren finally looked at his daughter and gave her the information he had been withholding all evening. "There has been an increase in the number of young men petitioning for wives, and so the village elders have decided to shorten the preparation time so as to accommodate the demand."

"So what does that mean for me?" she asked, almost afraid to hear his response.

"You now have only two weeks before you are to be presented before the petitioners and the village elders," he stated, dropping his head sadly. "I'm sorry. I wish all of this was not happening, but the decision has been made and we have no other choice, but to comply."

Stunned, Shoshanna studied her father's face. She could see deep lines of worry and sadness upon him, something she had never noticed before. Previously, she would have yelled and carried on as if her father could change what was being forced upon them all. Instead of responding in anger, however, Shoshanna felt a deep sense of peace wash over her.

Though she was beginning to understand there was a different way to live, her father still had no concept about the true freedom she recently experienced. He only knew what he had been told and believed what he had come to accept as normal. The way of the eagle and living in an uncommon manner was completely foreign to him.

Rather than anger, she felt a deep sense of compassion for her father. Maybe the time would come when she would be able to let him know the truth about their circumstances. But until then, she just had to continue assuming a position of submission. She couldn't reveal that she no longer feared the system.

Shoshanna was learning to operate in an uncommon manner as she followed the light directing her. She only continued her masquerade as a way to move around freely unnoticed by those who make it their business to report on the activities of others. For the sake of her freedom and her father's protection, she would need to cooperate temporarily with the plans of the village elders. Taking a breath, as if she saw no other way, she responded.

"Father, you know this doesn't give me much time to prepare, so I will need to take every free moment to finish my training. There may even be times when I will not be returning home at all, but rather staying late and beginning early so I can learn all that is needed for my presentation. Will you be alright with that?"

Oren's eyes widened at her request, but as he studied her calm demeanor, he recognized a new maturity in his daughter. Her ability to accept the distressing news he shared, and process it as quickly as she did, greatly impressed him. Though he was not excited about the idea of not seeing her each night, what she stated was true. She now only had two weeks to prepare when previously she had two months.

"If you would not be staying here, where would you be staying?" he asked wanting to verify her safety.

Noting her father's positive reaction to this new idea, she continued presenting her case. "I would be staying with the old woman who is training me, of course," she smiled confidently. "I know you are concerned about my safety, but I can assure you, I will be very safe as I focus on my preparations."

"So, where is this older woman and what is her name?"

Not wanting to expose Miss Haddie to any danger, Shoshanna carefully considered what she could tell him. Suddenly, the answer she needed came.

"We can just call her "the eagle lady" as she is often telling stories about these great birds while she is training me. She likes that name. As for her location, it would be really hard to explain which trails lead to her house without me showing you, and I know how busy you are these days."

Oren had to agree.

The quantity of both suppliers and customers coming in and out of his shop had greatly increased over the last several weeks. He really didn't have the time to go wandering through the woods on random trails to meet some old lady who was teaching his daughter how to properly care for a household. The time left for her training was very short. Without a wife to help prepare his daughter for this great change in her life, he felt he had no other option than to trust his daughter's own judgment to make the necessary choices in this matter.

"Alright," he agreed. "You can continue seeing this "eagle lady" for the remainder of the time before your presentation. I do, however, want to see you from time to time so I can find out how things are progressing."

"Yes, of course. You will see me. I do need to leave early tomorrow morning so I can inform my teacher of the changes." She paused for a moment before adding, "Thank you for having confidence in me."

With a smile, Oren walked over and hugged his beautiful daughter.

"You know this is going to be one of the hardest things I have ever gone through, next to losing your mother. I would much rather see you given to a worthy man than lose you forever.

Wrapping both her arms around her father, she buried her face into his chest breathing in the familiar smells of a hard-working man. She had no idea how long she could even remain under his roof. Her masquerade of submission would certainly be revealed at some point, especially if she did not appear at the presentation ceremony.

Until that time, all she could do was continue loving her father and learning all she could about this new way of living. Shoshanna did determine, however, that she would not let her father, and others like him, remain slaves without giving them a chance, at some time, to know the way of escape.

At this moment though, the truth would have to wait for the right time.

Chapter Seventeen

CLARITY OF DIRECTION

The two men had been walking and talking for some time before fatigue set in. With the prison a relatively safe distance behind them, they figured it was time to rest. Their escape had been very early that morning, and now the afternoon sun was peeking through the haze. Hunger was also becoming a factor. Galen and Uri had already missed the first two meals of the day. They had no food, but at least they could sit for a while before continuing on.

Surrounded by dense greenery, they felt fairly comfortable in taking a short breather once they located a suitable clearing. The temperature was a little cool, so Uri, the more experienced outdoorsman of the two, decided to build a fire to warm themselves by.

It didn't take them long to gather the branches and twigs they needed to get it started. Soon, a nice fire was burning so they could warm themselves while they rested. With the cover of the haze everywhere, they had no worries about their fire drawing any attention to their location.

Little was said as they stretched out on the ground close to the fire with the back of their heads resting on a fallen log. Just as they were settling in for a short nap, they heard rustling in the branches and the breaking of twigs nearby.

Assuming someone from the prison had tracked them to this location, they quickly hid behind the surrounding trees and listened. As the noise drew closer, Uri picked up a large branch just in case they needed some defense. Galen signaled his friend to hold still as they watched to see who entered the clearing.

Slowly a man approached the fire, obviously looking for someone. Just when Uri was ready to start swinging the branch, Galen suddenly recognized who it was. Roany! Without a moment's hesitation, Galen stepped out from behind a tree and greeted his friend. After excitedly shaking hands and patting each other on the back, Galen called Uri over to meet his friend.

"Uri, this is my old friend Roany. We have nothing to fear from him," Galen said smiling. With a wide grin, Roany stretched out his hand in friendship to Uri. Suspiciously, Uri eyed both Roany and his outstretched hand. He never was quick to accept a handshake. Deciding it was safe enough, Uri finally dropped the branch to the ground and shook his hand.

"So Roany, what are you doing way out here in the middle of nowhere?" Galen asked.

"Looking for you, of course! I've got something I need to tell you."

"Well, come on and join us at the fire, then you can tell us what's on your mind," Galen said as the three young men sat down on the fallen log.

"Before I do that, I have some things that may have been on your mind," Roany said while slipping the large knapsack off his back. The other two watched hungrily as Roany began pulling hard rolls, cold chicken, cheese, and apples from his knapsack.

Roany encouraged the two men to eat as he explained all that had happened in the village of Kieran since Galen and Uri's dramatic prison escape.

"First, let me say that when I discovered my mother was the one accusing you before the village elders, I was angry. I had no idea she planned to do that! I can't imagine what that was like for you with your arrest, the accusations, and then imprisonment. That must have been difficult for your parents to witness as well. I'm so sorry! My mother really meant no harm. She was just afraid for me and was trying to protect my future."

"I realize that, Roany. And I have already forgiven her," Galen responded. "But as you can see, Uri and I are doing fine, other than being a little hungry. We are out of prison and don't intend to go back. That is for sure!"

Uri nodded in agreement, but was too busy eating to comment.

Galen continued. "So tell us, what happened in Kieran once they discovered we were missing? How did you find us? And how did you happen to bring all this food with you?"

Roany paused, taking a sip of water from the gourds he brought to moisten his throat before beginning his full explanation.

"Once I learned of your arrest this morning, I told Jarek, the blacksmith, that I had some pressing matters I had to attend to and left. I asked around town to see if you were still in the prison. That's when I heard the reports of how the two of you had just vanished behind locked doors. By the way, that was quite impressive!" Roany commented. "You'll need to tell me how you did that later!"

Laughing, Roany proceeded. "So anyway, the whole prison is in an uproar even now. Every guard is being carefully questioned and apparently, none of them have any answers. They haven't even begun looking for you two yet!" he added with a smile.

"Oh, I did overhear them discussing some mystery woman who visited you in prison." Roany added. "They were thinking she might have had something to do with your breakout. So did she?"

Now Galen laughed. "No! Of course not. Don't be ridiculous!"

"Well, if she didn't help you, how did you lock the doors behind you?" Roany persisted.

Without even looking up from his food, Uri spoke up. "The doors opened and locked behind us by themselves."

Looking up for just a moment, he added, "I didn't do it," while glancing over at Galen as if to confirm his account.

Roany stopped for a moment to consider what they shared.

"Really?"

"Yes, really," Galen affirmed.

Shaking his head a bit in awe, Roany continued.

"Ok. So, once I heard you had escaped, I headed over to your parents' house to see if they had seen you. They hadn't, but your mother did mention that a young woman had come by and let her know that you were fine. Hmm. Could this be the same woman who visited you in prison?"

Galen thought for a moment. "Shoshanna?"

"Shoshanna? That was the girl at the prison?" Uri interrupted with a half grin. "Galen's wife, right?"

"She's not my wife, Uri! I told you that already!" He shook his head, a little annoyed at his friend's comment.

Under his breath, Uri spoke again. "She should be. Mighty pretty!" he added with a sheepish grin.

"Uri, stop! I want to hear the rest of Roany's story." However, it was too late. Uri's comments had already caught Roany's attention.

"So, who is this Shoshanna?" he asked, nearly bursting with curiosity.

Realizing that between Uri's comments and Roany's obvious interest, he would have to explain who she was.

"I just happened to meet her at Miss Haddie's one time," he clarified and then added a little hesitantly, "and I walked her home." Both Uri and Roany looked at each other with boyish grins. Roany pressed him for more details.

"We just talked on the way to her home. That's it!"

Uri, however, was eager to provide more information than Galen was wanting to share.

"She also brought us some great food while we were in prison," he added grinning.

Roany looked over at his friend smiling widely, "She brought you food? Nice friend."

"Okay you two," Galen interjected. "That's enough. I want to hear the rest of Roany's story. So, my mother told you about Shoshanna coming by. What happened after that?"

"Well, I told her you had escaped from the prison somehow and I was looking for you. Once she heard that, she loaded me up with goodies just in case I found you. That's it."

"And how did you know to look for me here?" Galen questioned him.

"Well, I remembered how we had always talked about exploring the smoking mountains sometime, so I figured I would start walking in that direction."

"And what about your apprenticeship? Are you planning on going back?" Galen wondered.

Dropping his head, Roany was reluctant to be transparent before the men, but he continued nonetheless.

"Actually, you were right, Galen. Being a blacksmith is not what I want in life. Honestly, I really hate it! I decided to walk away from it all and join you on this new adventure."

"Really?"

"Yes, really," Roany announced.

"And what about your mother?" Galen asked.

"She will have to learn that I am my own person and must decide things for myself."

"So, your mother doesn't even know you left your job yet?" Galen continued.

"I don't think so." Roany admitted.

Galen needed to caution him about the consequences of his choices. "You know, if you choose to join us, they eventually will be looking for you, too. We can never go back to how things were before. Do you understand that?"

"I do." Roany responded confidently. "I've thought it all through. I would much rather take my chances with you than have to face the hot furnace of the blacksmith shop day after day. I'm in all the way! But, I do think it might be wise for us to finish eating and continue on our journey. Where are we going?"

With this question, the full weight of responsibility he carried to lead this group hit him hard.

He was so busy talking to Uri about Elemet and the ways of the eagle that he had honestly forgotten to watch for the light directing his steps. They had just walked. And now he had no idea where they actually were. Just as he was about to admit he was lost, they all heard a man's voice calling out in the distance.

The three men grabbed their belongings, quickly doused the fire, and ran for cover behind the trees. As they listened in silence, they could begin to distinguish what was being called out.

"Galen! Uri! Roany!"

Bewildered the three looked at each other, stunned. How would anyone know the three of them were together at this remote location? Once again, Uri picked up a branch preparing to swing it, if needed. They made no movement, but waited to see if the voice would get any closer. As they continued listening, they noted that the voice was coming in the opposite direction from where Roany had just come.

"Galen!" the voice called out. "I have a message for you."

Curious, Galen motioned for his two friends to stay undercover as he decided to take a chance and see who this individual was. Slowly, he moved out into the open.

"Who is this?" he called back.

"Someone who can help you!"

Galen carefully scanned the horizon trying to catch a glimpse of any movement in the trees or on any of the many trails twisting through the forest. He saw nothing. Suddenly the man was standing right beside him. Startled, Galen tried not to appear shaken as he knew the other men were watching.

"I have some instructions for you," the tall, grey-haired man announced.

"Who are you?"

"I am known as Chen. I come from the Eagles' Nest. Elemet has sent me."

Seeing that Galen was conversing with the stranger, both Uri and Roany came out of hiding to get a better look. As usual, Uri came, but continued carrying a large branch in his hand, just in case. Undeterred, Chen continued speaking even as the men approached.

"There is one more person who is to join you before you head to the Eagles' Nest. You will meet this person at Miss Haddie's homestead before beginning your journey."

As his friends were still some distance away, Galen whispered, "I don't actually know where the Eagles' Nest is yet. Would you be able to direct me?"

Smiling, Chen respectfully responded, "When it is time for you to depart, you will see the light as you have in the past. I can also tell you to watch for markers along the way that will help you."

"Markers? What kind of markers?"

By this time both his friends were standing beside him. Chen nodded in acknowledgement of the two men, but continued with his directives.

"You will see eagles carved into the stone or wood around you from time to time. They are just indicators that you are on the right path."

As Galen gazed into Chen's eyes, he became mesmerized with the great depth of swirling blue light emanating from them. Shaking himself to stay focused, he continued his inquiry.

"And how do I start this journey after picking up the fourth person?"

"Head for the smoking mountains, and you will find what you are looking for. That's all I can tell you for now."

Glancing around at all three of the young men gathered before him, Chen continued. "You have been provided a place of shelter until the time you join with the fourth person, then you must begin your passage."

"The journey itself will test your endurance and to continue onward, you must remain focused on the important things and not let the peripheral things distract you." The three men looked at each other, wondering if they were actually ready for this type of journey. Chen proceeded.

"Fear is your great enemy and to conquer this, you must carefully guard both your thoughts and imaginations so they continue to agree with only what is true and good. I am confident that all of you will be able to make this journey successfully."

By this time, Galen was convinced that this man was someone very uncommon, one that he desired to know more about.

"Will we see you again?" he asked.

"Oh, I'm sure you will. For now, however, you need shelter and rest before you head to Miss Haddie's. If you will walk towards the hill behind you, you will find a cave with all the provisions you need."

The three men turned to look at the hill he was referring to and when they turned back, Chen was gone.

Taking a deep breath, Galen took the lead heading towards the hill. Uri dropped his branch once again as Roany grabbed his knapsack. There was not much conversation between the three as they were all still considering everything they had been told regarding this new journey before them.

It wasn't too long before they found the cave Chen had described with adequate bedding, fresh water, food and even a fire already warming their surroundings as they stepped in. They had one night to get refreshed before their visit to Miss Haddie. Beyond that, lay the greater journey to places previously unknown. It was an expedition that required all they knew and all they would soon learn in order to reach the elusive Eagles' Nest.

Chapter Eighteen

GIFTS OF MERCY

S everal days had passed since Yona's move to Ms. Bina's house and Jessah's flight with the golden eagle. Jessah still had the feather she had found in her bed following the adventure and took great pains to keep this and other treasures hidden from the prying eyes of others around her.

Remaining in Camp Shabelle, with its rigid rules and regulations, had become quite tiresome for the young girl. She had been given no further directions for any outside adventures in recent days. When she finally did hear from Elemet, she was thrilled! It was finally time for her to visit Yona's new residence with Ms. Bina. She couldn't have been happier!

All the new arrivals at Camp Shabelle had settled in their routine by that time. No one seemed to care much about what others were doing and eventually lost interest in watching Jessah's every move. She was both glad and relieved that their attention had been diverted in other directions so she could finally move about more freely.

After the second morning bell rang, the girls again assembled in proper order outside their door awaiting Miss Moselle's customary escort to their first classes. Jessah, in her position at the end of the line, anxiously anticipated the moment when she would be able to make her quick sidestep into the darkened hallway allowing her escape. She was ready to be released, at least for a time, from this confining world she had been forced to call home.

Finally, her opportunity arose.

Jessah made her move and seemingly "disappeared" from among the other girls without anyone even noticing she was gone. Her departure only required a few cautious moments as she negotiated her way to the hidden door leading to freedom outside the cold, stone walls of Camp Shabelle.

Though haze still encompassed the outside world, her path was well lit. Happily, Jessah moved among the trees of the forest. She was heading to a new destination: Ms. Bina's home where she and Yona would be reunited once again.

She could hardly wait!

While plodding down the path, Jessah carefully patted the small bag she had hidden under her clothing filled with all of Yona's personal items. Yona had been forced to leave everything behind at the time of her relocation. Jessah had concealed Yona's possessions for some time now and she was eager to deliver them back to her friend.

With Miss Moselle informing Yona that all her possessions would be destroyed at the time of her move to Ms. Bina's home, she naturally would have assumed everything she valued had been lost. Smiling, Jessah tried imagining Yona's expression when she first saw her lost treasures! Of course, along with Yona's belongings, she also carried her eagle feather. She could hardly wait to tell her friend about her own experiences as well! She only hoped they could speak freely during her visit.

Before too long, Jessah approached the outskirts of a village she had never visited before. The light directed her down a dirt road running alongside a few simple bungalows. No one was outside at the moment, but still, she proceeded with caution.

Eventually, the light rested upon a small, rustic cabin with smoke twisting and curling from its chimney adding to the smoky environment. Slowly, she inched her way up to a window allowing her to peer inside. Stepping up onto a fallen log nearby, her short frame was lifted high enough for her to see inside the home.

From her standpoint, she could see the back of a gray-haired woman sitting in a wooden rocking chair. The woman's wrinkled arms hung onto the sides of the chair as she gently rocked back and forth. A chipped and faded tea cup sat on a small, round table next to her with a few crackers sitting beside it. Jessah watched as the woman, whom she assumed was Ms. Bina, reached over and carefully felt around for the cup. Once her fingers located the handle of the cup, she slowly brought it to her mouth for a sip without ever turning her head.

Ms. Bina was blind.

As Jessah studied the frail woman, Yona entered the room. She recognized the love and compassion her friend showed to Ms. Bina as they conversed. Without making any sound, Jessah slowly lifted her head higher and higher in the window, so she could catch Yona's attention.

Yona, looking up from the woman, caught a glimpse of a face in the window and gasped in surprise. Quickly, Yona realized it was her friend smiling at her through the glass. After reassuring Ms. Bina that everything was fine, Yona gestured towards the back door where they could meet. Nodding, Jessah dropped out of sight. Moments later, the door swung open and Yona emerged. Neither of them said anything at first as they embraced.

Finally, Yona took a step back to get a better look at her dear friend. "I thought you had forgotten about me!"

"Never!" Jessah declared. "There is no way I would ever forget about you. I just had to wait until all the new girls settled in before I could leave." And then she remembered the main purpose of her visit. "Oh! I have something for you."

Reaching inside her garments, Jessah produced the bag she had carefully guarded for her friend.

"What's this?

"Why don't you open it and find out?" Jessah encouraged her.

Yona reached into the bag and pulled out several well-worn letters written by her parents to each other carefully folded, and a necklace with a polished green stone hanging from it. Tears of joy ran down her cheeks as Yona stared at the few precious reminders of her parents. It was all she had.

The grateful girl hugged Jessah tightly. Overcome with joy, Yona finally managed to get a few words out. Shaking her head in amazement, she asked, "How did you do this? I thought everything had been destroyed."

"Elemet directed me to the office where I overheard what Miss Moselle was planning," Jessah explained. "I was able to rush back to our room before anyone got there and rescue your things."

"Oh, Jessah! You are remarkable! These letters from my parents and my mother's necklace are very precious to me. Thank you!"

"You are welcome," Jessah replied. "Now, tell me how are things going for you here?"

"Actually, it has been quite wonderful living here with Ms. Bina! She even asked me to call her "grandmother" and treats me as if I was part of her family."

"Oh, Yona! I am so happy for you! This is certainly much better than Camp Shabelle."

"And how are things going for you there since I left?" Yona asked looking into her friend's eyes.

"Well, at first I was very sad about losing you. Elemet understood how I felt and wanted to encourage me. He actually had a wonderful surprise for me that night."

"And what was that?"

"After I went to bed, he met me and gave me a ride on a huge golden eagle!"

"What? How did he do that? Was it a dream?" Yona asked incredulously.

Smiling Jessah replied, "Well, at first I did think it was just a wonderful dream. But, then later, I found this in my bed." While speaking, Jessah pulled out the eagle's feather she brought to show her friend.

Gasping, Yona carefully touched the feather, stroking its smooth edges in amazement.

"It is so beautiful! You must tell me all about your flight and the things Elemet told you!"

Just then the two girls could hear Ms. Bina calling for Yona. They both realized the details of this adventure would have to wait for another time.

"I have to go now. But tell me, where you are going from here?" her friend asked.

"I'm not entirely sure, but I think I need to first visit Miss Haddie before I return to Camp Shabelle. I will definitely come by again when we have time to visit."

The two girls hugged once more just as Ms. Bina requested Yona's help a second time. Smiling, Jessah turned to leave while Yona walked back into the house. She could tell Yona was happy, and so was she!

As Jessah walked away, she knew she had accomplished what she had been sent to do. Now it was time for her to focus on the second part of her journey. While walking towards Miss Haddie's homestead, she quietly thanked Elemet for allowing her to be a part of this grand adventure.

Chapter Nineteen

AND THEN THERE WERE FOUR

t was quite early when Shoshanna left her home that morning. The paths leading to Miss Haddie's homestead had become quite familiar by now and it didn't take her long to arrive. As she entered the clearing, she saw Miss Haddie outside gathering produce and vegetables from her gardens and surrounding trees.

Though her heart was still weighed down by her father's news, she decided to lay that aside for the moment so she could assist her beloved mentor. After a quick greeting, the two worked together picking the ripened fruit and gathering assorted vegetables. The nearby baskets on the ground quickly filled up as the two worked in silence.

Finally, Miss Haddie spoke up. "Child, what is troubling you today? I can see it all over your face."

It didn't take long for Shoshanna to share the news her father gave her the previous night. Now with her preparation time cut short, she had many concerns about what this would mean for her.

"Though my father is saddened by the change, he is still committed to the idea of me going through with this. What are we going to do?"

"My dear, Elemet always has a plan and is not at all surprised by the changes. In fact, I believe he has already sent the answer in our direction." she continued. "Come, let's take our harvest inside, shall we?"

Together the two women gathered up the baskets and carried them into the home. Just as they were inspecting the harvest, a knock was heard at the front door.

Without even looking up from her careful examination, Miss Haddie called for the visitor to come in. Shoshanna turned to see Jessah standing in the doorway.

"Jessah! I have often wondered about you. How are you doing?" the young woman called out.

"I am doing fine. In fact, more than fine."

Miss Haddie washed her hands, walked over to the child and hugged her deeply, planting a kiss on the top of her head.

"How was your visit with Yona?" she asked while looking into the child's sparkling eyes.

"She is so happy in her new home!" Jessah exclaimed. "And I was able to return her personal items to her. It was so wonderful to see her again."

"Well done, child! You listened and followed directions perfectly! I have also heard something about a flight with an eagle?"

"Oh yes! Elemet took me for a ride on the back of a huge golden eagle! It was so beautiful flying up above Kumani!" Shoshanna's eyes grew wide in excitement at hearing this.

"Oh, please tell me about it. What did you see?" Shoshanna asked breathlessly.

Before she started, Miss Haddie directed both Shoshanna and Jessah to first sit down at the table. As they waited, both eager to proceed, Miss Haddie brought over tea and biscuits for the three to enjoy. Once everyone was served and Miss Haddie sat down, Jessah launched into her colorful description of her encounter with Elemet.

With great detail, she described what she saw while riding on the back of the eagle. As a dramatic ending to her story, the young girl produced the golden feather she had found in her bed afterwards. Shoshanna was in awe as she carefully stroked the feather with her fingers before handing it back.

After enjoying the biscuits and tea, Miss Haddie announced that all three of them would be working on food preparations that day. With delightful company nearby, the girls eagerly washed their hands, pushed up their sleeves, and began cooking a wide variety of delicacies.

Under the old woman's direction, the girls packed some of the prepared food as if they were going on a trip. The remainder of the cuisine was set out in preparation for a full meal. Both Shoshanna and Jessah wondered why there was such a flurry of preparation that day, but neither of them questioned Miss Haddie. They knew better.

With all the food prepared and ready to go, Jessah spoke up. "Miss Haddie, I loved spending time with you today, but don't you think I should consider returning to Camp Shabelle soon? They may be missing me by now."

Smiling, the woman approached Jessah, placing her arm around her shoulders.

"Actually, my dear. You have been given a wonderful gift from Elemet. All this time, he has kept you partially hidden from the eyes of those wanting to control you. However, as of today, he has caused all memories of you to be erased from Camp Shabelle entirely. You now have a different purpose."

"And what is that?" she asked with her eyes widening.

"Elemet has decided that I am in need of an efficient runner and messenger. He has chosen you to do that for me. That is, if this is alright with you."

"What does that mean?" Jessah asked, still puzzled.

"This means you can remain here with me rather than returning to Camp Shabelle. Is that something you would want?" Miss Haddie asked the child.

Without a word, Jessah threw her arms around Miss Haddie burying her face within her clothing for a time. Soft sobs could be heard as she struggled to gain her composure. Finally, she pulled her face away just enough to respond even as tears of joy flowed down her cheeks.

"You have no idea how often I dreamed that someday you might become my family! I am so happy, I don't know what else to say. Thank you, thank you so much!"

"My dear, I am thrilled with this change as well. I believe it will be good for both of us!"

"Yes, and I finally have a real home again!"

Tears welled up in Shoshanna's eyes as she watched the two embrace each other once more. They were so happy! She wondered if the day would come when she would be equally as happy.

Suddenly, the three heard a familiar voice calling outside the home.

"Miss Haddie! It's me, Galen. May I come in to see you?"

"Galen?" Shoshanna looked in surprise towards Miss Haddie.

"Oh, yes! I've been expecting him." Walking over to the door, Miss Haddie opened it to welcome the young man. "Galen! So good to see you. How has your adventure been since you left that terrible prison?"

Galen stepped inside smiling, but was a little surprised to see her other two guests as well.

"It has been quite interesting for sure! I see you have company today. Wonderful!"

He first walked over to Jessah to greet the young girl.

"And how are you doing, young lady?" he asked.

Jessah grinning broadly, responding quickly. "I don't have to live at Camp Shabelle any longer!"

"What? That is wonderful news! And where will you be living then?"

"Right here with Miss Haddie!" she blurted out excitedly.

"Is that right?" he asked while glancing back at Miss Haddie for a moment. Seeing her nod in agreement, he continued. "Well, that certainly will be a wonderful improvement for you. I can tell you both will be very happy with this arrangement!" Then turning towards Shoshanna, Galen continued his greeting.

"So wonderful to see you again! Now I can give you a proper thanks for coming to see me in prison. That food was wonderful!"

"Oh, thank you. I felt so bad about all that had happened. I was happy to do that for you," she smiled shyly.

"I also hear you were out visiting my parents as well," Galen continued.

"How did you know that?"

"That report came from a dear friend of mine. Actually, I have two friends waiting to meet all of you." Turning towards Miss Haddie, he asked, "Would it be alright with you if I invite my two friends in?"

"Certainly! I have been expecting all of you today. Bring them in."

Nodding, Galen stepped back towards the front door and whistled outside alerting the two men that they were welcome. Jessah and Shoshanna followed Galen outside with Miss Haddie closely trailing behind. They watched as the two men slowly stepped out into the clearing. Uri grinned widely as soon as he spotted Shoshanna again, but wisely decided to hold his tongue.

Galen stepped towards them and turned to introduce the men to his friends.

"This is my old friend Roany and my new friend, Uri who have joined me on my journey."

"Welcome, both of you," the old woman responded. "I am Miss Haddie. These two young ladies are Jessah and Shoshanna. Why don't all of you come in and enjoy a meal before you continue on your way."

Of course, the men gratefully accepted her invitation to eat as it had been quite a while since their early afternoon meal. The prepared food was ready, so they all gathered around the table to eat.

Each one of the guests had the opportunity to share about their lives prior to this gathering. All were in awe at the workings of Elemet in each of their circumstances. Everyone seemed headed towards a happy ending with the exception of one young woman.

Listening politely, Shoshanna tried desperately not to fret about her upcoming presentation. Although attempting to stay focused on the excited conversion buzzing around her, her mind kept going back to her approaching presentation getting closer and closer by the moment.

As the meal drew to a close, Galen's expression suddenly changed to a more serious look as he had to address one more topic. They had already discussed the mysterious appearance and disappearance of Chen and the directions he had given them. However, something else was still troubling him.

"So, I understand that Uri, Roany and I are to head towards the Eagles' Nest now. I am still puzzled as to why we needed to backtrack to your homestead before beginning our journey? Chen said there was one more person who was to join us. Do you know who that might be?"

"Actually, I do," Miss Haddie responded. "The group heading towards Eagles' Nest is not to be three, but four, just as you were told."

Shoshanna's head had been bowed down as she struggled to appear excited for everyone else, but when she heard the mention of a fourth traveling companion, she looked up in curiosity.

Miss Haddie continued. "Elemet has requested that Shoshanna join you on your journey towards the Eagles' Nest, if she is willing."

Both Shoshanna's eyes and mouth widened in surprise.

"The choice is yours, my dear. You can continue to live in an uncommon manner as you have been and take the risk of joining these men on their journey, or you can return to the life you lived before you met us. It's up to you."

Every eye was upon Shoshanna as she took a moment to consider her choices in this matter. Going to Eagles' Nest would undoubtedly mean leaving her father for quite a while and possibly never seeing him ever again. Her heart ached at that thought, but at the same time she knew she could never return to the darkness she once lived in. Taking a deep breath, she gave her answer.

"I have seen and experienced too much to be able to return to my old life. I am willing to go to Eagles' Nest. However, I was wondering if it is possible for me to say goodbye to my father before we leave? I don't want him wondering what became of me. He has already lost my mother and I don't want him thinking anything terrible has happened to me as well."

"I believe that would be fine, however, you must once again use great wisdom and caution when you speak with him. He cannot know the location or even the existence of the Eagles' Nest at this time. This is for his protection." Miss Haddie responded. "Can you do this?"

"Yes. I will only say what I am released to say to him."

"Good. Then these gentlemen will be happy to escort you first to your home and then onward to the Eagles' Nest." The three young men looked as each other nodding in agreement.

"There is only one more thing I need to ask about," Galen added.

"And what is that?"

"I have only been instructed to head towards the Eagles' Nest through the smoking mountains. I really don't know the direction I need to take."

Upon hearing this, Jessah nearly burst with excitement.

"I know where it is," she volunteered. All the adults stopped for a moment and looked at the child as she continued. "While I was riding on the back of the eagle with Elemet, I saw the Eagles' Nest from the air."

"Where was it located?" Galen asked hoping that she could recall its exact location.

"I saw it on the far side of this island in an area I had never heard of before. It was deep in the smoking mountains surrounded by high waterfalls, a wide river, and great cliffs. There was also one large bridge that seemed to be the only way to enter the Eagles' Nest. "

Roany spoke up excitedly. "We have always wanted to explore the smoking mountains and now we will finally have our chance!"

"Yes, but remember what Chen has already told us about our journey." Galen reminded the men. "He said it would test our endurance and that we must not lose our focus as we go."

With unusual wisdom, Uri added an important detail. "Didn't he also mention something about markers with eagles along the way?" At this, Shoshanna perked up as well.

"Oh! I once had a dream about an eagle carved in stone on a mountain path. The dream did not have a happy ending, but I do clearly remember what the carving looked like. That might be helpful."

Miss Haddie again spoke up. "So, my dears, I feel as though you have all been given what was needed to begin your journey, with one exception."

"And what is that?" Galen inquired.

"Food for the first part of your trip. Shoshanna, Jessah and I have already prepared what you need. It's time for us to load up your knapsacks so you can arrive at your next destination at the proper time."

At that point, the group arose and worked together dividing up the food equally in knapsacks for each of the travelers to carry. Once completed, the travelers turned, one by one, in thankfulness to the wise woman who was sending them off. The men each hugged Miss Haddie and then affectionately patted young Jessah on the head or squeezed her shoulder as she stood next to the old woman.

When it was Shoshanna's turn to say goodbye, she fought hard to subdue her emotions. She took a long moment to embrace the woman who helped bring a great change into her life. She had observed and learned much in the short period of time she spent around Miss Haddie. For that she was immensely grateful!

Next, she stood in front of the young girl who first led her to this wonderful homestead. Stooping down, she gazed into Jessah's bright eyes. Grabbing both her hands, she squeezed them affectionately. As she ran her hand along the side of her face, Shoshanna spoke with great love.

"Jessah, you are indeed an amazing young lady with an incredible future. I am so glad you finally have a real home of your own. I couldn't think of a better place for you to be." Then looking up into Miss Haddie's face, she continued. "I hope that this will not be the last time I see either of you, and in the days ahead, we might be together again, if Elemet allows it. Thank you for loving me."

With that, Shoshanna hugged them both again and turned to join the men who were already heading towards the door. As they walked in the direction of the path, they could see that the sunlight was growing dimmer by the moment. It was important for them to arrive at their next destination before nightfall.

The group stepped onto the path towards Shoshanna's home. One last time, she glanced back to see if Jessah and Miss Haddie were still standing in the doorway waving. As she watched, the forest itself seemed to enclose around the entire homestead causing it to disappear from sight.

She had seen this before, however, this time she understood it was one of Elemet's methods to protect those he loved. With renewed focus, she and her three companions moved quickly towards Zera so she could see her father one last time.

Chapter Twenty

A GROWING THREAT

Deep in the forest region somewhere between the villages of Zera and Kieran, elders of both villages filed into a large darkened room. A fire burning in the chimney created the only light in the room. Wooden chairs carefully placed in a large circle awaited the arrival of the anticipated guests. A lone hooded woman standing next to the door greeting the hooded figures as they filed in, one by one and took their seats.

Once all were settled, a man stood to address the gathering elders.

"Good morning, my fellow elders from the village of Zera. We, the governing elders of Kieran, welcome you. We have called for this assembly together to discuss a growing problem which, we have learned, has come to include some residents in your village as well. We all know how important it is for us to carefully guard and protect our way of life so as to prolong our ability to survive on this island," he said while looking at each of the men surrounding him.

"It has been brought to my attention that two of our imprisoned dissenters have recently escaped from our enclosure in Kieran. Now I am hearing that another of our young men suddenly left his assigned position of apprenticeship. He has not been seen since.

"His mother, in concern for her son, has graciously researched her son's sudden disappearance and has come back with some valuable information for us. What she has learned may be helpful in allowing us to locate both her son and the escaped dissenters. At this time, I would like to invite Tanzi to disclose what she has uncovered."

The hooded woman standing in the corner somberly stepped forward and drew back her hood allowing all the men to clearly see her face.

"I am here this morning to reveal what I have discovered about the disappearance of my son, Roany," she began. "First, I do want the elders from Zera to know that I am the one who first reported the rebellious activities of a friend of my son. Once the elders were informed of this negative influence upon my son, the man, Galen, was arrested at his parents' home. After standing before the elders, Galen was taken to our enclosure while his final fate was to be decided."

"While imprisoned, Galen and another prisoner, Uri, escaped; though I still do not understand how this happened," she added while glaring at the elders of Kieran. Still without answers, the men glanced uncomfortably at each other as Tanzi continued.

"After the prisoners escaped, I came to learn that my own son had abandoned his apprenticeship position. I am convinced that his behavior was directly linked to the influence of Galen. My son was temporarily swayed by the words of this man. He is responsible for misguiding my son, causing him to neglect my own wise counsel and wishes of the village elders."

Horrified, the men spoke excitedly among themselves discussing the problem that had arisen, but Tanzi quickly interrupted.

"I am not finished!"

The men once again turned their attention to the woman standing before them.

"After learning of Roany's sudden disappearance, I decided to visit Galen's parents to discover if they knew anything about this. Though they claimed they had not seen their son, I did manage to find out that a mysterious young lady came to visit them soon after Galen's arrest. His father divulged her name as Shoshanna. By asking around the various villages in our region, I found that Shoshanna lives in the outskirts of Zera with her father, Oren, your local butcher, I believe."

The tension level increased as the men attempted to place blame on each other for not monitoring things more diligently. Tanzi called them to attention once more.

"Gentlemen, I must conclude my report before you discuss things any further." Quickly, the assembly quieted down again allowing her to resume.

"I have learned this "Shoshanna" has been added to your list of eligible ladies in the village of Zera. I suspect that this young woman has something to do with Galen and

Uri's escape and my own son's disappearance as well. They may have all joined ranks and could be traveling together. It is my suggestion, that the wise elders of both Zera and Kieran assemble all their resources together very quickly to descend upon this young woman's home before all of them disappear out of our reach."

Once Tanzi concluded her presentation, the men exploded in rage towards the audacity of these young adults trying to destroy and ruin their way of life. The volume level of the rabble increased until finally, the first man arose to bring order to the crowd.

"Gentlemen, gentlemen! Calm down! Everyone calm down so we can discuss what actions must be taken in this matter. It is obvious that whatever is decided here, we must act quickly in order to snuff out this rebellion before it spreads to others in our villages."

Though the voices decreased, the fervor and rage did not subside as Tanzi stepped back into the corner near the fireplace. She was obviously quite pleased with herself at the urgency she had stirred up within the elders. Of course, her main concern was retrieving her son from the grips of the rebellion he had been sucked into.

Roany has always been way too impressionable and even gullible in regarding the words of his friends, she consoled herself. Maybe this dramatic rescue will bring him to his senses so he will not lose all that he has already worked for.

It wasn't long before the elders had devised their plan of action. Shortly, they left the gathering place to begin assembling their enforcers. Time was of the essence! It was their intention to quickly descend upon Oren's home in hopes of capturing the dissenters.

Chapter Twenty-One

HONORABLE CHOICES

There was yet a bit of sunshine peeking through the haze on the horizon when Galen, Uri, Roany and Shoshanna arrived in the village of Zera and stood in front of her home. Smoke arose from the chimney indicating that her father had already returned home from his job. Shoshanna stepped out into the clearing while the young men stood back undercover.

For several moments, her eyes carefully examined her one and only home since childhood. She recalled all the fun and precious moments she shared there with her parents prior to her mother's death. The free and untroubled days of her youth had vanished as all the forced changes and requirements fell upon her now as a mature, young woman.

All the events leading her to this place ran through her mind. She had come to see things quite differently now. Learning of Elemet had activated many new things in her life. No, there was nothing drawing her to return. She had to be strong and make her intentions known to her father, though he would likely be heartbroken.

Wisdom told her she could no longer live under fear and tyranny. She had tasted and seen the way life could be and loved it. Things could never be the same.

Taking a deep breath, Shoshanna stepped towards the door, just as it swung open. Her father stood there in silence. He was already sensing his daughter had come to some kind of a decision that he was not going to like.

"Shoshanna! Are you coming in? I've been watching you stand outside for some time."

"I was looking at our home and remembering all the wonderful memories of my childhood," she responded. "We really had some sweet times in those early years, didn't we?"

"Yes, your mother was amazing and made this place a real home." With a sigh, he stated what he already knew was true. "You're not coming back home, are you."

She had a hard time looking him in the eyes as she considered what she could say.

"Father, I can't stay. I am going to another place on this island where I will be allowed to live and love freely. I won't submit to being paraded in front of others so they can choose what they want, leaving me with no say in it at all."

Oren stared at her as tears welled up in his eyes.

"Your mother and I were happy. Things worked out for us, until she departed," he admitted. "Please don't go. You're all that matters to me in this village."

"If I matter to you, then you would want me to be free to make decisions for myself. I can't do that here any longer. I have to go."

"But how can you leave your home when you are all alone?"

Looking back towards the shadows hiding in the forest behind her, she responded, "I'm not alone."

At that moment, Galen, Uri, and Roany stepped out from the trees revealing their presence. Oren was surprised as he looked over the young men standing before him. Shoshanna continued.

"I can't tell you exactly where we are going, but I can promise you that I will be honorable and pure just as you and mother taught me. My life is different now. I'm not afraid any more. "

"Will you be married then?"

"I may marry someone at some point in my life. However, not right now. If I do choose to marry, it will be in a manner that shows respect and honor to all."

Glancing back again at her three friends still standing behind her, she added, "And don't worry. I will be safe and protected during our journey."

"Will I ever see you again?" Oren could no longer hold back the tears.

Shoshanna walked up to her father and embraced him. It was quite some time before she was able to speak. "I hope that I will be able to see you again. I have so much to tell you about. I have learned a lot and it has drastically changed how I see the world and there is still so much more for me to discover. I can promise I will make every effort to come and see you when I can."

Once again the two hugged silently until Shoshanna released him to join her friends.

"I love you, Father."

"I love you as well." Then looking sternly at the young men standing behind her, he spoke with authority. "I am giving you charge of my daughter to escort her to the place she is speaking of. I trust that you will guard and protect her on this journey."

Galen, taking a step forward, replied, "Yes sir. We will take care of her and bring her safely to our destination."

"Thank you," Oren replied.

Just as the group was about to leave, an angry mob began approaching the house with torches and chains in hand. Spotting the foursome, the enforcers rushed towards them. Galen, Uri, Roany, and Shoshanna turned running into the forest behind them with the rabble close behind. Just as the group entered the foliage, huge thorn-filled bushes began rapidly growing obstructing the mob from following the young adults into the forest. Several men carrying axes chopped away at the thorny hedge, but even as they chopped, the briers seemed to grow back in even greater abundance.

Not willing to give up on their pursuit, the crowd turned back deciding to look for another entrance into the forest where they might be able to overtake the rebels. However, before they all left, the leader of the pack turned towards Oren threatening him.

"We will be back to interrogate you later. If you know what's good for you, you will not withhold anything you know about this!" Angrily, the man turned away to follow after his companions.

Oren stood outside his home staring for quite some time at the now darkened woods surrounding him. With the recent threats still ringing in his ears, he carefully considered all that he witnessed. Obviously some other power was at work protecting and guiding these young adults in their pursuit of freedom. Was there something beyond all the control and fear he had lived under for so long?

It was now evident that both his home and his life would never be the same. He realized that even with the little Shoshanna shared, it was time to consider if there might be different way for him to live as well. Without a wife and a daughter to fear for, he saw that much of their control was already beginning to wane. Rather than fearing their threats, he discovered a new courage rising up within him. He now felt a new longing to know more about this life his daughter spoke of.

Her courage and the courage of her friends inspired him.

With other options quickly vanishing, he came to the one remaining choice. Maybe it was time for him to go wandering in the woods himself. Maybe it was possible that he would be led to this "eagle lady" who had obviously trained Shoshanna in much more than mere household duties.

Yes, he had seen the forest close up before the mob, but possibly the forest would not block him. Perhaps this power which protected the young people would see his desire to investigate this new way of life and allow him entrance.

Oren turned back into his home realizing that he only had a short time to gather what he needed before the throng returned. Grabbing all the camping supplies he owned, his plan was to enter the forest and then camp out for the night. At daybreak, he would begin his search for the old woman who held the answers he needed.

Once he had gathered supplies, he put out the fire, and stepped outside. Before leaving the clearing, he glanced back once more at the rustic cabin he had called home for so many years. With smoldering smoke still streaming out of the chimney, he suddenly realized that things had changed within him. His desire to save and hang on to his previous life had completely evaporated.

No longer did he feel pressed to hang on to his little corner of the world. He was free. Though he knew he could not pursue his daughter, he somehow felt that something much bigger than him would guide him to the answers he sought.

Taking a breath, Oren stepped up to the thorny briers still blocking the way into the forest. Closing his eyes, he decided to step into the thorns to see if they would yield to him. As he stepped forward, he felt no pricks at all. Opening his eyes, he realized that he had successfully entered into the safety of the woods. The dense thorny hedge was now behind him.

Breathing a sigh of relief, he looked up and silently thanked the power that had allowed him to escape as well.

As his eyes adjusted to the darkness of the forest, he thought he saw a flicker of light in one direction. Not knowing what else to do, he decided to follow the light to see where it might lead him.

Meanwhile, Shoshanna, Galen, Roany, and Uri were beginning their journey of hope as well. They now knew with certainty they were being pursued. This knowledge added a sense of urgency to their journey, but at least they knew Elemet was actively guarding and protecting them on their way.

The first thing on all their minds was to find a safe place to sleep for the night before beginning their journey into the smoking mountains. They knew better than trying to master the mountain trails at night. As they trudged forward, Galen felt most responsible for the decisions before them. The light was clearly directing them, so they followed and asked no further questions. Elemet knew what was needed.

Though Shoshanna kept up with the quick pace set by the three young men, her mind was clearly on the father she had left behind. Though they had been delivered from the mob, her father would now have to face the anger of the village elders himself. She knew he had not tried to stop the escape of the foursome. She tried not to let her imagination lead her thoughts into fear and worry for him.

He is a smart man and can figure out how to avoid the enforcers, she consoled herself.

Realizing there was nothing she could do, she focused on staying close to the other three people while carrying her own knapsack.

It wasn't long before the group noticed another light, much brighter than the one that was leading them, emanating from the forest ahead. Galen signaled for all of them to stop, as he wanted to explore before inviting the others to follow. Unfortunately, Roany and Uri would have no part of it and Shoshanna refused to be left behind, so they all moved ahead with caution.

As they approached, they saw a small clearing with multiple tents set up around a blazing fire. Remaining in the shadows, they scanned the area looking for any kind of movement. As they stood momentarily hesitating, Chen suddenly stood beside them. Shoshanna nearly screamed at the sight of a stranger in their midst, but Galen quickly assured her that Chen was fine.

"Come in, come in, my friends," he assured them. "I have been expecting you," Chen said with a smile. "I see you were successful in picking up your other companion."

"Yes, Shoshanna has joined us." Turning towards Shoshanna, Galen introduced her. "Shoshanna, this is Chen. He is from the Eagles' Nest and I imagine we will see him from time to time as we get closer to our destination. Right?"

"Oh yes, you will see me at times during your journey," Chen responded. "Greetings, Shoshanna! I am so glad you have joined them. And may I assure you that your father, Oren, is also being taken care of, so you have nothing to fear."

"Thank you so much for letting me know! I was very concerned about him. Can you tell me what he is going to do?" she asked.

"Unfortunately, my dear, I cannot give you the details of his journey. Just know he is being led by the same light that now leads you. Your job at this moment is to simply focus on your own journey so you can gain all that is needed in the days ahead. However, this is the time for each of you to relax and get refreshed here for the night. Creation will cover you just as it guarded you earlier this evening. Observe."

With that Chen looked upward and as he did, the surrounding trees began to swell in size. New branches and foliage created an impenetrable wall of protection around them.

"You will be safe here," he reassured them. "Come now and get settled, for tomorrow the real adventure will begin." With that comment, Chen stepped up to the dense trees and appeared to pass right through them, vanishing from their sight.

Wide-eyed, the four companions moved towards the tents before them. Little was said as they laid down their knapsacks and unpacked the food they carried with them. The peace of Elemet descended upon them like a warm blanket while they sat around the fire eating. With full stomachs and a warm shelter, the travelers retired to their tents for the night. They had full assurance that whatever lay ahead of them, they were not alone in their pursuit of the mysterious Eagles' Nest.

ABOUT MARY TRASK

Mary Trask is first and foremost, a lover of Jesus Christ, a wife, a mother of four grown children, and a grandmother of six incredible grandchildren. Her passion is to teach and encourage others around her to be all they were created to be. Though a gifted speaker and teacher, her joy has been to relay stories from both her own experiences and the experiences of others.

www.heartreflectionsministries.com

mary@heartreflectionsministries.com

She is also the author of two other books: "The 12 Gemstones of Revelation" and "Weapons of Peace" which are available for purchase from numerous online sources.

"Flying with the Eagles: A Way of Escape" is the first in a series of "Flying with the Eagles" fiction books.

CPSIA information can be obtained
at www.ICGtesting.com
Printed in the USA
FSHW021634120219
55616FS